You and Me

By

Jade Winters

You and Me

By Jade Winters

Published by Wicked Winters Books

Copyright © 2021 Jade Winters

www.jade-winters.com

ISBN: 979-8-595-70733-6

Other titles by Jade Winters

<u>Novels</u>

No Other Love
Falling
All That Matters
Missing Pieces
143
Caught by Love
Guilty Hearts
Say Something
Faking it
Second Thoughts
Just One Destiny
Unravelled
Picking the Right Heart
The Second Time
Secrets
In it Together
Love Interrupted
The Song, The Heart
Accidentally Together
Flirting with Danger
Unravelled
Lost in You
Starting Over Again

<u>Novellas</u>

Talk Me Down from the
Edge

<u>The Ashley McCoy
Detective Series</u>

A Walk into Darkness
Everything to Lose

<u>Amber Hills Series</u>

Love's Knocking
Always You

<u>Looking for Ms Right
Series</u>

Looking for Ms Right
Torn
The Chase

Chapter One

The late evening sun shone through the large bedroom window, casting a warm glow in the reflection of the floor to ceiling glass wardrobes lining one side of the wall. The spacious room, once filled with memorabilia, was now nearly barren. Gone were the framed photos of happier times which usually hung on the walls. As were the books which took pride of place in the homemade bookcase, filled with topics ranging from politics to real life crime and titillating romance novels. Now the room was plainly furnished, all signs of Alice gradually disappearing, pretty much like she would be shortly.

'Alice?'

Alice's body straightened into an upright position. Just hearing Izzy's voice took her back to a place she didn't want to be.

Into reality.

Today of all days, she could do without it.

Alice didn't turn around, instead, she remained focused on the job at hand – neatly folding a pile of clothes and putting them carefully into her large suitcase that lay open on the bed.

Tentative footsteps neared, as if in slow motion, taking an age before finally coming to a standstill behind Alice. She imagined Izzy's forlorn expression as she took in what Alice assumed was her pathetic-looking figure hunched over her case.

Although Izzy had broken Alice's heart into a zillion pieces and more, she didn't want to label Izzy a bitch. Was she a self-centred person who only cared about her own happiness? Who knew? The simple truth was that they both wanted different things out of life. Alice totally got that. Better to tell the truth than live a lie.

And the truth that Izzy had to get off her chest? That she had fallen in love with another woman. A co-worker.

How cliched!

Shit happened, Alice knew that, but she hadn't expected it to happen to their relationship.

Izzy's footsteps started again as she moved around Alice and sat on the edge of the king-sized bed, her fingers twisting around one another in her lap.

Izzy bowed her head in Alice's peripheral vision. Alice tried her best not to make eye contact because if she did, she might just release the tears that were presently blurring her vision. That was something she would not give Izzy the privilege of seeing.

I'm in love with another woman. The words refused to cease looping in Alice's mind. Her Izzy, her soulmate, had found love with someone else. The shock still pervaded her body, her mind desperately seeking answers to unresolved questions Izzy refused to entertain.

How long had their affair been going on?

When they'd made love had Izzy thought of her? Of them?

When had Izzy realised she no longer loved her?

Did she ever love me?

Life could change as quick as a flick of a switch, as Alice was now witness too. One minute she'd been in what she'd thought was a long-term committed relationship, the next, she'd been summoned to sit down at the dining table in the kitchen as Izzy wanted to 'talk'. Izzy's declaration of love for her colleague, Judith, had come out of the blue.

The once comforting vision Alice had held in her mind of them growing old together, tending their small garden while the other looked on, was now a distant dream. Obliterated back into the unknown void from where it manifested.

In the present moment, every sound, every tiny movement was now intensified in the bedroom. This was the finale. The point of no return.

'So is…' Alice paused momentarily, unable to complete the sentence, her heart not wanting to know the answer.

'Is?' Izzy pressed after a few seconds.

'Is she going to move in with you?'

Izzy laughed spontaneously, though it quickly faded upon realising its inappropriateness.

'No, we want to take our time, you know, considering the circumstances.'

'How nice for you both.' Alice let the sarcasm drip from each word.

'Come on, Alice, try and understand… it wasn't my fault. Things just kind of… happened?'

'If not now, when?' Alice said, closing the lid to her case with a sense of finality.

'What?'

'It's a Buddhist saying. It just seemed apt for the occasion. If you didn't cheat on me now, when would you have? Next week? Next year?'

'This is why I can't talk to you.' Izzy's eyes narrowed, her taut expression scolding Alice.

'So this is my fault, is it? You fuck another woman and I'm the one that should be silenced?'

The words were out before Alice could stop herself. If Izzy had any sense of compassion or empathy, she should understand why Alice would lash out. This was the last time Alice would be standing in this room, and it hurt knowing it was all because of something that was no fault of her own.

'You know I'm just as upset as you are, Al.'

'Yeah, I'm sure you are, but hey, you get to move on to a nice shiny new toy now, don't you? I wonder how long it'll be before you get bored of her.'

'Alice, we've been together two years and we're still no further on than we were when we first met.'

A red-hot dagger pushed through Alice's heart would have been less painful than the words Izzy so carelessly spoke. Yes, their relationship was in the midst of a storm, but it was one that Alice thought they would eventually pass through and emerge into bluer skies, like they always had, but to say they hadn't moved on in all that time? Had Izzy been living under a rock for their entire relationship?

It seemed when it came to picking women, sound judgement and good sense abandoned Alice.

'Not moved on?' Alice asked, dumbfounded. 'What exactly should our relationship look like right about now?'

'I duun—'

'No, you don't 'cause you're talking crap! You want out and that's fine, but for fuck's sake, spare me the insults.'

Izzy quickly backtracked.

'OK… so what I mean is that we've grown apart. You at least agree with that?'

Alice bit her tongue. Izzy's absences for increasing lengths of time had been a bone of contention for a while. Though she was loathed to admit it, her own workload may also have been a contributing factor to the distance between them.

'It's irrelevant now anyway. It is what it is.'

Alice's stomach tightened. If she didn't leave their flat soon, she would throw up there and then. She'd kept a lid on her emotions for days now, ever since Izzy had delivered her 'revelation', and they were now in danger of boiling over.

'You know there's no rush for you to leave today. I've got a three-day conference this week, so won't be here. Find somewhere nice first, huh?'

'I can't stay here,' Alice explained, her voice now wavering for the first time.

Gradually, over the past few days, the atmosphere in the flat had become insidiously toxic. Blame games were played out endlessly, night and day, hence the need to escape before things got any worse, and words were spoken that could not be unsaid.

Though Izzy didn't deserve her restraint, what was the point of letting things drag on? It wouldn't be good for Alice's state of mind, and that's what she had to protect now, more than anything.

Izzy stared up at her as she continued to pack. 'Are you staying with Stella?'

Alice shook her head. She knew Stella, her best friend from school, would welcome her with open arms, but she would want to know every single detail of what had transpired between Izzy and herself, and that was something Alice wasn't ready to talk about. Not yet anyway.

'I spoke to Emily. She said I can crash there until I get myself sorted.'

Izzy frowned. 'I thought she'd be the last person you'd want to be around, especially now.'

Alice shrugged nonchalantly, but Izzy was right. Contacting her twin sister after such a long period of time had been a tough call to make, but given her present circumstances, there wasn't an appealing alternative. Unless of course Alice considered holing up in a hotel, where she'd spend her nights alone, giving her ample time to dwell on the fact that yet another relationship had suffered the family curse of not surviving the long haul.

While Alice was skilled at presenting an image of a well put together person, the sad fact was that she wasn't, and hadn't been for a long time.

The failure to be happy and experience a sense of contentment was rampant in her family genes. As was the inability to feel whole – *complete*. Maybe she was destined to be alone forever. Standing there with her world crashing down around her, it certainly felt like it.

'I'll just have to suck it up for a while,' Alice said quietly.

Alice pulled the zip closed on her last suitcase. Her thoughts now moving to her immediate future. There was no doubt in her mind that Emily would want to talk about the past upon her arrival, despite Emily knowing exactly why Alice had stopped returning her calls. Emily being Emily, she'd still press for answers, but she'd be wasting her time. Alice wasn't in the mood to talk to anyone about anything, so Emily was going to be sorely disappointed if she was under the impression they'd be having a sisterly chat any time soon.

Izzy reached for the suitcase handle. 'I'll help you—'

'No!! I can manage.' Alice didn't mean for her tone to be as sharp as it sounded.

Izzy held her hands up in surrender.

'OK, well, I guess this is it then?' Izzy rose from the bed, causing the case to bounce just a little.

'Yep. I guess it is. I'll come back for the rest of my stuff when I find a place of my own,' Alice said, taking one last look around the room. The very room, that up until an hour ago still contained most of her belongings. The dark wooden chest of drawers, normally covered with her toiletries, was now bare.

Opening her handbag, Alice retrieved a bunch of keys and, with trembling fingers, removed the key to Izzy's flat and placed it tentatively in the palm of Izzy's hand. It was quite a contrast to the day Izzy had first given it to her. Back then, there had been tears of joy, whereas today the ones she successfully blinked back were those of sadness.

Alice gazed into Izzy's eyes, desperate for an inkling of regret. Instead, the look of relief reignited the fiery stabbing in Alice's belly that had eased a little overnight but hadn't completely disappeared.

She can't wait for me to leave.

Izzy nodded. 'I'll box it all up ready for you.'

Alice grabbed her case, dropped it onto its wheels, and headed to the door without looking back.

She didn't know the etiquette for saying goodbye to a cheating ex-partner.

Chapter Two

'What you lookin' at, Kerry?'

Kerry quickly swiped away the site she'd been checking out on her phone. 'Just the weather forecast.'

Pushing herself to her feet, Kerry headed over to the worktop where the kettle was in the nurse's break room. She flicked it on to boil, then spooned in a teaspoon of coffee while her brain worked overtime, calculating how much money she would need to save.

'How's it lookin'? Bit miserable out there today,' Debbie, her colleague and best friend, asked.

'More of the same for the next couple of days,' Kerry said, hoping the forecast she'd seen on TV that morning still held good.

'Oh, well. Spring's comin'. It can only get better. You up for goin' out for a drink when our shift ends?'

Kerry had known Debbie since they both started work on the same day after finishing their degrees. In some ways, she envied her. Debbie had a boyfriend she'd set up home with. A nice family that Kerry had met a couple of times when she'd been invited to barbecues, and her life set in a pattern Debbie seemed to be happy with.

On the other hand, Kerry was anything but sorted on the happy life front. No girlfriend in sight, living alone in a two-bedroom flat close to the hospital, and now with a desperate urge, an itch that she'd been scratching at for a couple of years which simply refused to go away, no matter what she did or how she tried to take her mind off it.

Kerry had thrown herself into work, even more so than previously. Working on a cancer ward in a major London hospital was hard on the emotions, but she loved caring for her patients. Looking after people, providing some solace for them at a time in their lives when they, and their families, were at their lowest ebb, fitted right in with her personality.

Kerry was a ray of sunshine, she'd been told often enough by patients to believe it was true, and she loved her work, but the last few months, the smile had faded a little, the ready quips became a little less ready, and the words of comfort, a little more difficult to find for her because of her distraction.

It was something Kerry always wanted, but the timing never seemed quite right, more pressing matters always taking priority.

All Kerry wanted, and needed in her life, was a baby.

At thirty-four she wasn't getting any younger, and as the cliché goes, her biological clock ticked louder with every day that passed. The thought of holding her special baby in her arms sent a warm glow through her, closely followed by a cold stab of fear through her heart.

The main obstacle was the cost. Kerry had been researching exactly that on her phone when Debbie interrupted. The fertility clinic charged thousands of pounds. While her savings would cover the first set of fees, how could she afford to raise a child?

Given Kerry's outgoings and limited income – being well into her overdraft at the end of each month with no real back up should something disastrous happen – her circumstances weren't the best of starting positions. The final goal of having a child would of itself necessitate some major financial changes, so yet again it seemed like the wrong time.

And yet…

Kerry knew it was going to involve sacrifices. She knew that financially it probably wasn't the smartest of moves.

And yet…

That urge was there. Undeniable. Irrevocable. All-consuming.

To ignore it had proved impossible.

To tell herself time and again that it would be a disaster had only made the longing worse.

Every time she saw a small child laughing and playing, her heart filled with joy. Every baby's cry brought a lump to her throat.

Her whole body, indeed, her whole self, cried out that she needed to do it. It wasn't a choice anymore. It was a necessity.

Kerry tipped water into her cup and spent a minute mulling over her quandary but getting no further. She needed to talk it out with someone and there was no one better than Debbie.

'A drink would be great,' Kerry said with a smile.

'Good. The Badger's Arms?'

'Perfect.'

The local pub would be quiet when they arrived. The ideal opportunity to get it all off her chest and hopefully find a way forward.

A little ball of excitement burst into life inside her.

***

'How was your shift?' Debbie asked, linking arms with Kerry as they exited the hospital's main entrance.

Kerry thought back to waving goodbye to a patient heading home, having had good news about her treatment, then in the next moment having to be a pillar of strength and a shoulder to cry on for the wife of a patient who'd been told his cancer was terminal and that the doctors could do no more for him.

'Pretty ordinary,' Kerry said, not wishing to burden Debbie with the emotional toll she was carrying. Debbie's own work in the paediatric ward was just as sad, if not worse at times.

'That bad, huh,' Debbie asked knowingly, glancing at Kerry with her deep brown eyes.

Kerry nodded. She'd spent more than enough time in her role to understand the vagaries of nursing. It was part of the job, Kerry knew that. It was hard, but over the years she'd become skilled at enforcing personal boundaries to protect herself.

'Well, that's why pubs were invented and put next to hospitals.'

Kerry laughed. A new retail park had been built

just before the hospital. It included the requisite pub, to service the tired, thirsty and hungry among the shopping fraternity. It was also eminently handy for a quick after work drink for the hospital staff.

When they pushed through the main doors, the warmth inside the bar was in marked contrast to the chill outside. Kerry took off her jacket at the table while Debbie ordered drinks through an app on her phone.

The aroma of fried food filled the air. Kerry's stomach rumbled as she sat down but she was unable to tell if it was hunger or nervousness that had prompted the reaction.

'Blimey, Ker, sounds like you need to eat too. What d'you fancy? My treat. Kev got a big bonus at work last week so I'm flush at the minute, and I'd sooner spend it on you than let Kev buy any more fishin' gear. We've got enough piled up in our garage to start a bloody tackle shop already.'

'Maybe you should go with him?' Kerry said as she scanned the menu. Nothing grabbed her attention, but Debbie was right, she was hungry and was grateful for Debbie's generosity.

'What d'you take me for? Sittin' in the bloody freezin' cold all night waitin' for a bite. I can think of better places to be on a chilly night,' Debbie said with a wink.

'I know. Hot bath, clean PJs, a fluffy dressing gown, and crappy shows on the TV?'

'Exactly. Add in a decent gin and a bit of a cuddle and that, my friend, is the perfect night.'

Kerry couldn't help but join in with Debbie's laughter. She was always so happy and content with her lot in life. Kerry had to wonder why she couldn't be the same. What primeval urge was tempting her to throw her life into the air and hope the pieces all fell back in some kind of order?

'I'm havin' fish 'n' chips,' Debbie said decisively.

'Sounds good to me.' Kerry returned the menu to its holder while Debbie finished off the order on her phone.

The next couple of minutes were spent passing on inter-hospital gossip about a particularly good-looking junior doctor and a frontally well-endowed nurse who seemed to have gained his attention.

'I mean, I know he doesn't do anything for ya, Ker, but a lot of the female nurses, and some of the male staff too, are gettin' a little hot under the collar about him.'

Rumours of a semi-naked tryst in a storage cupboard were doing the rounds, and the two of them laughed at some of the wilder speculation about them both.

Once the drinks then the food arrived, the talk turned to less salacious topics until they had finished, and Debbie treated them both to another drink.

'So,' Debbie said, 'what's goin' on?'

'How d'you mean?' Kerry asked, feeling a tiny stab of nerves inside.

'I mean you. You've been mopin' around at work for the last few weeks, and when you've not been mopin', your face's been plastered with the fakest smile I've ever seen. So out with it. What's up?'

Kerry stared into her glass for a few seconds, plucking up the courage to tell Debbie the truth, then deciding to go for it.

'I want a baby.' Kerry wouldn't tell her the whole story behind it. Not yet. She had to be sure it was going to happen before she revealed all.

Debbie spluttered the mouthful of drink she'd just taken, back into the glass. 'Bloody hell. A baby?'

'Yeah. Don't sound so surprised.'

Debbie's expression turned to one of incredulity. 'On your own?'

'Yes, Debs, on my own. Plenty of other people do it, but there's a problem.'

'Just one?' Debbie joked, having recovered her equilibrium.

'Ha-ha, yeah, I need to earn more money in case the first round doesn't work. Not to mention support myself when the baby's born.'

Debbie let out a soft sigh. 'Well, you won't manage that on a nurse's salary.'

Kerry shook her head. She'd worked that much out for herself.

'But—'

Kerry jumped in. 'Yeah?'

'Give me a chance to finish. Why don't you look at private agency work? Last time I checked, there were plenty of jobs. I bet they'd snap someone like you up.'

'Really?'

'Yeah. You're a good, experienced nurse. Why wouldn't they? Plus, you'll be able to choose the hours you work once you've had the baby.'

For the first time since Kerry had really begun to focus on the possibility of having a child, she thought, just maybe, she might be able to do this.

Chapter Three

Slamming her foot on the accelerator, Alice drove as fast as she could, away from the split-level Victorian flat that was no longer her home. The sudden continuous downpour of rain that beat ferociously on her windscreen, blurred the surrounding buildings as she sped past them, only stopping when a red traffic light forced her to.

Tears drenched her cheeks as she sat waiting for the light to turn green. Her hands clutched the steering wheel, her knuckles white.

Alice didn't know how she'd managed to keep it all together back at Izzy's, but she had. What did her mother always tell her? *Never show your emotions – people will just think you're weak.*

Her mobile pinged in the phone holder and she tapped the screen.

Please drive carefully.
I'd never forgive myself if anything happened to you x

Alice snorted. Who the hell was she kidding? If Izzy cared about her in the slightest, Alice wouldn't be in the situation she was in right now, driving around the streets of London like a bat out of hell. She deleted the message only for her phone to ping again seconds later.

I meant what I said. I really do hope we can be friends.

No point in us throwing two years down the drain for nothing.

For nothing!!!
Alice didn't know how to reply to that, or whether such an insulting message warranted a response. In the end, she decided it did. Even if it was petty.

I didn't throw anything away. You did that all by yourself!

Not wanting to get involved in a text message war with her, Alice switched off her phone and drove the rest of the way to Emily's, silently fuming at the cheek of the woman.

The last spots of rain fell from the dark laden skies just as Alice removed her cases from her car and wheeled them up the path to Emily's front door.

A brief hello was followed by a silent twenty second walk along the elegant hallway, a large chandelier illuminating the winding staircase. Emily showed Alice into the spare room, where Alice was going to be spending the next few weeks, and silently closed the door behind her.

The room was different from the last time Alice stayed. Emily had only just moved in then, and much of the house needed renovating. The bedroom was now dominated by a king-sized bed covered with silk bedding. On the wooden floor lay a large multi coloured Persian rug. Oak rustic shelves held books and ornaments, and the air was scented with the aroma from fresh flowers sitting idly in a slimline crystal vase.

Catching sight of herself in a gold gilded mirror on the antique dressing table, she hoped Emily hadn't noticed her puffy, swollen red eyes. Though to be fair, they were hard to miss. They stood out like a pair of beacons in the night.

Grabbing her toiletry bag from one of the cases, Alice took out a pack of facial wipes and cleaned the faint traces of mascara from her cheeks.

She'd been in her room barely five minutes before there was a gentle tap on the door.

'Come in,' Alice called out, trying to sound light-hearted even though the total opposite was true.

The door opened but Emily made no attempt to enter, instead, she opted to linger in the doorway, moving from foot to foot under her weight. It never failed to amaze Alice how strange it was to see another person who looked exactly like her. Emily's dark hair was worn in a bundle of thick luscious curls on top of her head, pretty much how Alice always kept her own. They both had cute little button noses, as their dad used to call them, and curved lips conveying an ever-cheerful disposition. The only tell-tale difference was a small mole above Emily's lip.

'So are you going to tell me what's happened?' Emily's pale blue eyes bore into Alice's before darting around the room and resting on her suitcases.

Alice couldn't pretend everything was normal. If it had been, she would be at home, probably cooking for one, not sat in her sister's spare room, surrounded by all her worldly possessions. The truth was Alice didn't actually know what to say. How to explain to Emily that her partner had cheated on her without looking like a complete and utter fool. Emily would no doubt want to know how an affair could have taken place without Alice having even an inkling. She just hadn't. Not a single clue until Izzy dropped the bombshell on her.

'Can we not do this now, Lee?' Alice's mouth was dry. She sucked her tongue in an attempt to stimulate some saliva, just so she could talk properly. 'Any other time, just not now.'

No matter how disconnected their relationship was, Alice still called her sister Lee, a nickname from childhood, a time when Emily was her hero. It still disturbed her to think how quickly Emily had turned into a villain in her eyes.

'You're just like Dad,' Emily said with distaste. 'Never wanting to talk about things.'

How many times throughout their childhood had Alice heard their mother make the same complaint to their dad because he'd just got home from work and arguing over trivial matters was the last thing on his mind.

'And you're like a broken record,' Alice shot back immediately.

'So it's going to be like this, is it?'

'Like what?' Alice rubbed her eyes to stop the prickling sensation behind them. If she didn't want to cry in front of Izzy earlier, there wasn't a chance in hell that she was going to shed a single tear in front of Emily.

Still staring at her, Emily shook her head, loosening several ringlets which she roughly stuffed back into her hairband. 'D'you know what? Forget it. I'll talk to you in the morning when you can be civil.'

With that, Emily pulled the door closed and her footsteps sounded down the hallway until they finally faded.

Jesus Christ! If I'm like Dad, she's definitely like Mum. Nothing's ever enough for either of them. I don't think they'd be happy even if I gave them every drop of blood from my veins.

It was strange, whenever Alice saw Emily, she triggered memories of their mother's poor treatment of her growing up. Maybe it was because Emily had been the only one to really witness it.

Alice's throat constricted at the memory, as if someone had their hands gripped around her neck, making it difficult to swallow. Just the thought of Carol withholding love from Alice but lavishing it on Emily, who was completely indifferent to her, evoked a physical reaction.

All of her senses heightened, Alice sat on the bed with her eyes closed, feeling as small and vulnerable as she had as a child. She recalled the countless times she'd tried to please her mother, even spending the thirty pounds she'd saved to buy a special present for her mother's birthday, only to find said present in the recycling bin the following week. Alice had been heartbroken, but she hadn't said a word about it, not wanting to upset her mother. She wanted, no needed, desperately to believe the ornament had been thrown away by accident.

Even back then, deep down in her heart, Alice knew it wasn't the case, but she suppressed facing the truth – that her mother knew Alice had seen the gift as she'd specifically asked Alice to look in the bin for something she'd allegedly lost. There was no denying the look of victory in her mother's eyes when Alice had returned inside. Alice had only been seven years old, and up until this day she could not understand why her mother had acted so cruelly.

Yet, as always, Alice felt a pang of guilt whenever she questioned her mother's motives. It wasn't her mother's fault after all, and she really wasn't horrible all of the time. Alice had to remind herself that her mother's upbringing had been awful. As she told Alice time and time again, if she had never been loved, how would she know how to show it?

Too tired to unpack, Alice undressed, climbed into bed and sprawled out on her back. After such a stressful day, Alice thought it unlikely sleep would come easily, but to her surprise, as soon as she closed her eyes, she found herself drifting, her eyelids growing heavy by the second, her breathing shallow and then…. The alarm on her phone screeched from the bedside cabinet. Alice opened her eyes and groaned at the display – five a.m. Had she really been asleep for nine hours?

Alice knew better than to ignore it. Hitting the

snooze button for another ten minutes would only lead to a continuous cycle and she'd never get up. Throwing back the cover, she climbed out of bed and made her way along the hallway to the bathroom.

Sliding out of her night shirt, Alice stood naked as she turned on the shower. Her nipples immediately hardened, and goose bumps covered her arms when the icicle air made contact with her skin. Alice stepped into the hot steaming shower, tilting her head upwards, the full force of water pelting down over her face, gradually descending over her body. She scrubbed vigorously, hypothetically washing away the past as the grey cloudy water swirled in circles beneath her until it disappeared down the plug hole.

Back in her bedroom ten minutes later, Alice dressed in a tailored black suit and white shirt, tied her hair up in her trademark bun — easy and, she liked to think at least a little stylish — and checked herself over in the mirror. Thirty-four. Where had all those years gone?

She ran her fingers gently over the lines at the corner of her eyes. Laughter lines, although when she thought back, there hadn't been a lot of laughter for a while in any aspect of her life. She'd plucked the first grey hairs from her head a couple of weeks before, but now she looked again, there were at least a handful of them shining brightly under the light.

Alice wandered down the stairs after applying a thin layer of makeup to her face. She only had time for a quick coffee before leaving for work. The only saving grace of Emily's home was its proximity to a tube station.

After what seemed an interminable journey, combined with a quick stop off for another strong coffee from her favourite café close to the office, she stepped inside the elegant reception area of Travis & Elliott's Trades and made her way to her office on the tenth floor. Ten minutes early. She breathed a sigh of relief.

Then she opened her e-mails.

Fifteen minutes later she was in the plush office of her boss.

Twenty minutes later, she had been fired.

Alice couldn't remember more than a few words he'd said to her, but it amounted to her underperforming, which she had been for months. Apparently, she'd lost her hunger. There were hundreds of keen, younger people who would kill for her job. She'd had a final warning a month before and nothing had changed so…

Alice walked out of the building an hour after she'd entered, with a cardboard box containing the meagre possessions kept in the drawers of her desk.

As she sat in the café, sipping on a cappuccino, the feeling that her life was slipping away, collapsing around her ears, washed over her, and try as she might, tucked away in the darkest, furthest corner of the café, she couldn't stop the tears streaming down her cheeks.

Chapter Four

Sitting in front of her computer in her compact and orderly office at the back of her house, Emily stared at the blank screen, then absentmindedly raised her head to look out of the window at the garden which resembled a golfing green. She'd reached a dead end mentally. She was by no means a stranger to writer's block, but this was something else. Something much more serious. The overwhelming sadness inside her eclipsed anything she had ever experienced before.

Alice's call out of the blue seeking refuge had given Emily hope that they'd be able to repair their broken relationship. She'd missed Alice. Not having her in her life felt like she'd lost a part of herself, but their first encounter in over a year had been a disaster, and it wasn't all down to Alice, as Emily had been just as defensive in her approach.

Emily noticed her sister's red swollen eyes as soon as she'd opened the door to her, and Emily didn't know how she'd made it through the brief conversation with Alice without embracing her.

I accused her of being like our dad.

Emily cringed at the thought. Alice was nothing like him and never could be in a million years. So why had she let rip at her like that?

Because that's what she did when her back was up against the wall.

It was obvious Alice had only reappeared in her life because she had nowhere else to go, and it cut to the bone.

Refocusing to concentrate on the job at hand, Emily typed a few words, read then deleted them. *No point in writing stuff just for the sake of it.*

Thankfully, she was halfway through the biography she was penning, so there was no need to rush, as her editor knew she'd 'come up with the goods' as Fern called it.

Most importantly, she'd deliver what was required of her on time.

The goods. Fern made it sound as though the memories were something Emily had stolen, which couldn't have been further from the truth. All of the information in her possession had been left to her by the man himself – Clyde Bridges. The once most sought-after actor of his time.

Womaniser.

Drunk.

And one more addition to the list Emily was ashamed to admit – father to herself and Alice.

Father? What a joke! To the general public who loved nothing more than reading about his real-life antics off set, Clyde was a source of entertainment, but for Emily he was nothing but an embarrassment. How many times had she endured the humiliation of Clyde being totally legless in front of her friends, who would laugh and spread vicious rumours about him the next day at school?

His past was a tragedy in itself. Clyde had been on the straight and narrow before Emily and Alice were born. As far as she could tell from the notes, he had been content being a husband to their mum, Carol, but as soon as fatherhood became a reality, it seemed playing a doting father was the furthest thing from his mind. In all honesty, Emily couldn't understand why he simply didn't leave the family home sooner than he did.

Emily slipped her reading glasses back onto her nose and forced herself to focus on the last paragraph she'd written.

It was a sad recollection about a great woman she'd never met but wished she had. Her grandmother Elsie Bridges, who had died just after Emily and Alice were born.

By the way Emily's father had written about her in his notes, it was clear Elsie had been his rock. The rod that held the family of ten together.

He respected her. Looked up to her.

So why had he treated their own mother with such coldness? And more importantly, why had Carol put up with it?

Because she was weak, that's why.

Yes, Emily was still bitter. She couldn't help herself. Each time she recalled hearing her parents argue from the bedroom next door, something inside Emily died just that little bit more. By the time she left home at eighteen to attend university in Scotland, any residue of respect for her mother had been erased.

Emily walked out of the family home with one

suitcase and a lifetime of memories she hoped would fade, but they hadn't, and she didn't think they ever would until she faced her demons.

And facing them she was.

Emily had no intention of sugar coating his image. The public would get the truth about the man behind the fake smile and jovial manner. Emily was going to make sure that everyone knew what a cheating bastard Clyde Bridges was.

Even if it meant losing her sister forever.

Chapter Five

Alice was still reeling from the shock of being fired. Her emotions were on a bumper car ride of random thoughts dashing around aimlessly in her head, colliding with the next, then going off in a totally random direction altogether until the next inevitable collision.

Though three days had passed since she officially became unemployed, Alice still checked her phone and email religiously in the hope that her boss would call her and say it was all a dreadful mistake, and could she come back as soon as possible, but that elusive call or email never materialised which meant only one thing – Alice had to come up with plan B. She couldn't keep pretending to go to work each day. The strain of wandering around London like a lost soul for eight hours was starting to wear thin. The fact that she couldn't, or wouldn't, tell Emily what had happened, only proved to her how distant they had become. At one time they had shared everything, from their closest secrets to the mundane. Now they shared nothing.

The reason they'd reached this point had all been down to Emily as far as Alice was concerned. The fact that Emily hated their parents wasn't an emotion Alice shared, even though neither of them were in contact with their father in the end. On the other hand, things were different when it came to their mother. That was one connection Alice couldn't sever.

Out of respect for Emily, Alice honoured her wish and refrained from sharing any family news that pertained to their mother. Up until a year ago, Alice had easily kept her part of the bargain, but then their father suddenly died.

In the midst of her grief, Alice thought Emily would come to realise how short life was and let her grudge go, but his death had only served to make Emily dig her heels in deeper. Not only had Emily refused to attend their dad's funeral, but she'd not been to see their mother once. Then Alice heard about the biography and their relationship immediately soured.

Their dad was dead. He had no way of defending himself from his grave. Alice thought it cowardly of Emily to reveal his secrets to the world instead of confronting him when he was alive. When Alice pointed this out to Emily, her words hit a brick wall. There was no getting through to her, and if the past few days were anything to go by, it didn't look like Alice ever would.

Alice's mind ceased its continuous whirl and started to gather together the first tendrils of a plan.

First things first. No ties.

That meant no relationships, at least for a while until she got herself sorted out.

Second. *Never become complacent in my next job.*

That was a given. Alice had stupidly thought she was an asset to the company, when apparently, she was far from it.

No, from now on she had to look out for number one. No one was ever going to fuck her over again. Alice would only do what she wanted. Live how she wanted to live and take no prisoners. And she would most definitely not apologise to anyone for her change of heart.

What would please her now, would be to jump on a plane with no destination in mind and just take each day as it came.

Alice always said she would like to travel, but had never found the time, and if now wasn't the perfect opportunity, then there never would be one.

Once Alice had left for 'work', she settled herself in at a café with her laptop, a plate of toast and jam, and a pot of tea.

First things first.

Alice checked her bank balance. She'd never felt the urge to blow all her money on expensive nights out in swanky bars and restaurants like many of her younger, predominantly male, colleagues did. After ten years and several guilt inducingly large bonuses, her savings account had a healthy five figure balance. That had certainly been a major factor in her lack of desire for a new job, although if she decided to buy a home and pursue anything more than a spartan lifestyle, that situation would change rapidly, but at least for now, there was no need to rush into anything.

Alice clicked away from the blank screen and googled 'world travel', spending the next few hours checking out tours that took in some of the places she had always dreamt of visiting. They were enticing. So much so, that with a few final clicks as she took a bite out of a chocolate cake, she had booked a trip around the world for a year that took out a large chunk of her savings. When the confirmation e-mail came through, she leant back, almost forgetting the stool was backless.

A sense of satisfaction replaced one of uncertainty. After three days of essentially moping around, she'd now begun to take back control of her life.

A year long trip would be the making of her.

It would give her a chance to think about exactly what she wanted to do next, both in terms of her immediate future and more long-term.

Alice gazed out of the window, her vision blurred by the downfall of rain that lashed against the pane in a wild frenzy. She could just about make out the red lights of the cars outside, bumper to bumper. The way traffic in London came to a near standstill when it rained was ridiculous. Another reason she would be glad to see the back of the city.

Having achieved her one aim of the day by late morning, Alice found herself at a loose end. Although she bemoaned having to stay at Emily's for another two days before her flight, Alice was still grateful for Emily's hospitality in putting her up during such a tough period in her life.

Maybe it was time to pay back that generosity and do something nice for Emily by way of a thank you. So far, they had managed to skirt around the elephant in the room and stick to meaningless chatter. Surprisingly, they both seemed content with things that way.

Alice decided now was as good a time as any to tell

Emily that she'd packed in her job to travel the world. Although it was a small white lie, it would mean Alice wouldn't have to fend off a million questions she had no desire to answer. The humiliation would be too much to bear.

Alice packed away her laptop, drank the last dregs of lukewarm tea and headed for the exit.

A trip to the local supermarket produced the necessary ingredients sadly lacking in Emily's kitchen, and by late afternoon, just as Emily returned back from her meeting with her editor, pans were simmering on the hob and the aroma of garlic filled the air.

'What are you doing?' Emily wailed as she walked in through the door, straight into the unruly mess covering every worktop. Tidiness was not Alice's forte, especially when it came to cooking.

'Cooking dinner.' Alice wiped her forehead with her wrist to try and dislodge several stray hairs that had slipped out of her bun.

'But… we don't… I mean I don't… oh my God, look at all the mess, Alice!'

Emily leant on one of the breakfast bar stools doing her best impression of a fish out of water gasping for breath, her mouth opening and closing with strange groans emitting as she cast her eyes over the carnage Alice had made in Emily's expensive, but ultimately, underutilised kitchen.

'Don't worry,' Alice said, scared Emily was going to put a massive dampener on the lightness of spirit she'd been feeling all day. 'I'll clean it up when I'm done.'

'But… but… but… the mess. You know I hate mess.'

'And I told you, I'll clean it up,' Alice said, determined not to let Emily get to her.

'You can't. You shouldn't… shouldn't…'

'What? Just get it out.'

Alice could feel an outburst coming on. Emily shook her head, seemingly trying to marshal her thoughts.

'You can't just come in here and do this… Look at it.' Emily waved a hand around at the unkempt kitchen.

The sink was full of dirty dishes, and batter encrusted cutlery lay on the flour covered worktop. In Alice's attempt to prepare salad and batter pieces of cod, she had used nearly every available plate and utensil. Empty wrappers she'd forgotten to bin were still strewn across the kitchen table, giving the impression of being messier than it really was. Ten minutes tops and she would have it spick and span.

Alice knew it was yet another trigger from living in their untidy childhood home, despite both their best efforts to keep it clean. After their father moved out, the house seemed to be in permanent disarray. It was as if their mother thought she could somehow punish their father, who was meticulous about cleanliness, a trait Emily seemed to have acquired, by refusing to clean.

'Look, why don't you set the dining table. I bought a nice bottle of merlot. Have a glass and relax. By the time I'm finished, you won't even know I've been cooking,' Alice said, trying to reassure her.

Alice's phone vibrated somewhere under the empty packaging on the worktop. Emily located it, gathering the wrappers as she did, and passed it to Alice.

'Hello?' Alice said, accepting the call and eyeing Emily as she frantically tided the worktop.

Before Alice could utter anything other than 'yes' to confirm she was Carol's daughter, the caller informed her of an incident that had taken place.

Alice listened carefully and thanked the caller when she'd finished. She looked over at Emily, trying her hardest to keep her emotions in check.

'I know you probably don't want to hear this, but Mum's had a stroke.'

Through tear blurred eyes, Alice saw Emily take a mouthful of wine. She said nothing for a few seconds, then…

'I'll clean the kitchen.'

Alice gave a curt nod in return. Message understood. Not even a stroke was enough to melt Emily's ice-cold heart.

Never had Alice thought she would meet someone who could be so callous and lack compassion for another human being.

That was until now.

Chapter Six

The cosy seating arrangement softened the otherwise formal outlay of the Harmony Nursing office. Large, framed images portraying caring nursing staff aiding elderly clients adorned the delicately shirred rose satin wallpaper, giving the impression that the agency put the care of their clients first. An ethos Kerry was more than happy to sign up to.

'Bloody hell, I hate paperwork,' Kerry muttered to herself, forgetting where she was for a moment.

Esther, the agency's supervisor, laughed. Her gold rimmed glasses perched firmly on her aristocratic nose giving her a scholarly look. 'Don't let the boss hear you say things like that. Record-keeping, as I'm sure you know only too well from your nursing experience, is something we all have to do, like it or not.'

Kerry took the point in what she hoped was the spirit it was intended and smiled.

'I know. It's the bane of our lives but a necessary evil.'

'Indeed,' Esther said, sliding the form Kerry had just completed over to her side of the desk and flicking through the information, nodding as she read.

'That's great. You're happy with the pay?'

'Yep, it's perfect.'

'Fantastic. Now normally we'd ease you in over a few weeks, but we're exceptionally busy at the moment, so you're going straight in at the deep end I'm afraid. I'm sure you'll cope just fine. I had a new client come in this morning. Her mother had a stroke.' Esther removed her glasses and rubbed the bridge of her nose with her thumb and forefinger before replacing them. 'Thankfully, it was a mild one and she's been released from hospital, but her daughter wants a nurse on hand to administer medication and do night observation just in case anything happens again.'

'I can imagine. How many days?'

'A family friend is a nurse and looks after her but can only do Monday to Thursday. So, Friday to Sunday is all yours if you want it? For now, it'll only be for a month, then the family will reassess her recovery.'

A month would be a good starting point to squirrel away some extra money. As well as this, Kerry was already working four days a week at the hospital so a weekend shift would fit in perfectly with her schedule. 'I'll take it.'

'I'll give the client a call. She may well want you to start today,' Esther said with a broad grin. 'I'll let you know the details ASAP.'

Kerry returned the smile, grabbed her bag and headed to the door.

'Have a good day.'

'You too,' Kerry replied over her shoulder.

Night shifts would be right up her street. It would help in alleviating the loneliness she often experienced. Although it wasn't as all-consuming as it used to be, it was hard getting used to sleeping alone after sharing a bed with someone for so many years.

When Kerry thought of all the times she'd moaned about Sarah pulling the cover off her in the middle of the night, she cursed herself. She'd give anything to have that back now.

Kerry arrived home and immediately made her way to the hallway cupboard, grabbing her overnight bag in case she was required to work that night. In her compact bathroom, she was halfway through filling her toiletry bag when her mobile phone rang. She fumbled in her pocket for it then accepted the call.

'Hello.'

'Hey! How's it goin'?'

'Oh, hi, Debs. I'm just packing.'

'Goin' somewhere?' Debbie said.

'Yeah, possibly a shift from the agency,' Kerry tucked the phone between her ear and shoulder then zipped the bag closed.

'Wow, that was quick.'

'That's what I thought but they're really busy, so in at the deep end I go.'

'You'll be amazin'. Let me know how it goes.'

'Yeah, of course I will.' Kerry walked out of the bathroom and into her bedroom next door. 'I'll text you later.'

'OK, and good luck.'

'Thanks. Speak soon.'

Without thinking, Kerry pulled open the oak wardrobe door and almost immediately her breath caught in her throat. This was the first time in a long while she'd looked in that side of the wardrobe. Had she not been so distracted with thoughts of work, that mistake would never have happened. It was too late to turn away now and her eyes were drawn to the row of clothes neatly hung up next to each other. Kerry willed herself to be strong. To remember that they were just clothes - *her clothes.*

Unable to stop herself, Kerry quickly leant forward and buried her face in a cashmere jacket. Her heart dropped to her stomach upon smelling the faint scent of her perfume still clinging to the soft material. She pulled the jacket from the hanger and took it over to the bed with her, still pressed firmly against her face.

Perching on the edge of the mattress, Kerry reluctantly released one of her hands in order to pick up the framed photo on the bedside cabinet, laying it down on her lap. Sighing heavily, her fingertips traced the outline of the smiling woman staring back at her, the moody sky in the background adding a beautiful backdrop to what had been a perfect day.

'I miss you so much.' Kerry closed her eyes, her fragile heart ached, the eternal pain never ceasing to erode. As she drank in the image of the woman she'd loved more than life itself, Kerry thought of the day they'd exchanged forever rings on top of a Ferris wheel.

Though Kerry was afraid of heights, the magic of the moment eclipsed her misgivings. As the car ascended, the sun set behind the sea, casting a warm glow across Sarah's delicate features. Sarah retrieved the ring from her pocket, gently placing it on Kerry's finger as they reached the apex.

'I love you,' Sarah had said, 'you make me feel on top of the world.'

To others it may have sounded cheesy, but to Kerry it was one of the most perfect moments of her life.

And they had been on top of the world for a while. Before it had all come crashing down around them.

Before the usual deluge of tears could fall and give vent to the agony of her loss, Kerry's phone rang again.

She checked the ID – unknown. Thinking it might be the nursing agency, Kerry accepted the call.

'Hello.'

'Miss Nicholls?' A male voice said, bright and chirpy.

'Yes, yes, that's me.'

'Great, this is George from Vodaphone, your mobile provider. I was just wondering if you realised—'

'Oh, not now,' Kerry said as the emotions caught in her throat sounded as though she was struggling to breathe.

Although it had been five years since Sarah died, every now and then it still hit her with the same enormity as if it were yesterday. That the woman who had completed her had slipped peacefully away in her arms.

Suddenly caught up in the unfairness of life, Kerry swiped away the call and slammed the phone on the table, then quickly checked she hadn't smashed the screen in anger.

The screen indicated a call-in progress. She snatched the phone and put it back to her ear.

'Look, I don't care which company you're from, I just want—'

'Kerry,' a female voice spoke, sounding more than a little perturbed.

'Oh sorry, Esther, yes it's Kerry.'

'Oh good. I thought for a moment… well it doesn't matter. I've just spoken to the client, Alice Bridges, and she's happy for you to start this evening.'

'That's great,' Kerry said, her spirits lifting.

After falling back into the abyss of grief yet again, Kerry desperately needed to put some space between herself and the bedroom. No, it was more than that. It wasn't space that she needed.

You have to pull yourself together and move on.

Kerry could only achieve it by removing all traces of Sarah from her flat, otherwise she'd remain in a perpetual cycle of sorrow. Sarah wasn't coming back. She'd never slip into her clothes and have Kerry compliment her on how good she looked. Kerry would never see that bright smile radiating from the photo ever again.

Kerry made a promise to herself that she would bag up Sarah's belongings and take them to the charity shop the following day.

'Good,' Esther said. 'I'll text the address over in a minute.'

'OK, brilliant, thank you so much.'

'You're welcome. I'm sure you'll be a great match.'

And with that Esther was gone without waiting for a response.

***

At precisely five minutes to ten, Kerry turned onto Wakefield Road, the address Esther had texted her earlier. Along the quiet oak tree-lined road, streetlights projected a feeble amber beam down onto the pavement.

Kerry pulled up outside a gloomy semi-detached house. It stood in stark contrast to the surrounding houses. Its unkempt front garden was littered with broken furniture and black rubbish bags. The window frames gave the impression they hadn't been repainted since the house was built – dirty white paint flaked away exposing the wood beneath.

Kerry grabbed her bag from the passenger seat and climbed out of her car, mindfully walking up the unsteady path to the large, but equally neglected, black front door. She pressed the discoloured white doorbell and absent-mindedly inspected the exterior of the house while waiting.

The downstairs windows were dusty and festooned with decaying cobwebs. The brickwork at the side of the house was shackled with thick untamed ivy.

She pressed the bell again.

No response.

Should she ring again and risk sounding as impatient? Rather that than being deemed late.

Kerry's finger hovered over the doorbell uncertainly, then she turned her head, resting her ear against the door. Nothing. Not a sound.

'Hello.'

A woman's voice from an alley at the side of the house caused her to jump and squeal, dropping the overnight bag she was carrying.

'Oh, I'm sorry. Did I scare you?' the woman said as she took a few steps forward.

Dark hair and a wide smile greeted Kerry under the security light that had been tripped.

'J… just a bit,' Kerry said as she bent over to pick her bag up off the floor.

'Are you Kerry?' The woman looked her up and down.

'I am,' Kerry said, slowly starting to regain her poise.

'I'm Alice.' The warmth of her smile echoed in her voice.

'Carol's daughter?' Kerry asked. 'Nice to meet you.'

Kerry held out a hand which Alice took in her own. Their handshake lingered a moment too long causing Kerry to hastily draw her hand back and drop it to her side.

They stood in silence for a moment, heat slowly making its way up to Kerry's cheeks.

Unnerved, she didn't dare look at Alice to see if she had noticed the effect her touch had elicited. Kerry stuffed her hand in her jacket pocket and made a mental note not to shake hands with Alice again if it was going to leave her feeling this flustered.

'Come in,' Alice said with a bright smile as she pushed the front door open. She turned briefly and looked down at Kerry's hands but said nothing.

Kerry followed Alice inside, gently closing the door behind her. The interior was no better than the exterior. Upon entering, newspapers and flyers were stacked up on an already cluttered table. Bald patches in the threadbare carpet led to unvarnished wooden stairs. A rickety lopsided floor lamp, solely responsible for lighting the hallway, stood pitifully in the corner. The walls were covered in faded blue wallpaper, though the design, if there ever had been one, was no longer visible.

Alice gave a nervous laugh. 'My mum has a problem with change.'

Kerry smiled politely but said nothing. She wasn't there to judge how anyone lived. Her job was to care for her patient. Simple as that.

'Mum's asleep now,' Alice said, gesturing for Kerry to follow her upstairs.

Kerry couldn't help but notice how compelling Alice's eyes were. Such a pale blue they almost look translucent.

'How is she?' Was that a tremble in her voice?

Alice gave a slight nod as she reached the landing. 'She's doing really well. Thank God it was only a mild stroke. The doctor said with her meds and plenty of rest she'll be back to her old self in no time.'

They walked along the hallway in silence, then

Alice opened a door at the end very slowly. She stepped aside to let Kerry enter.

Putting back on her armour, she was Kerry the nurse now. Professional. In control of her emotions. In this role, she would never allow herself to be taken by surprise. She was ready for anything.

'I know I'm being overprotective by hiring a nurse rather than a carer but I'm paranoid in case she has another stroke and I somehow miss the signs.'

'It's totally understandable,' Kerry said, thinking back to when Sarah had been near the end of her life and the numerous checks she had performed to make sure she was still breathing.

Stepping over the threshold, Kerry took in the woman lying in the small double bed as she moved closer. Her greying blonde hair hung loose over her shoulders and her expression was one of peace. Probably because she felt safe in the knowledge that she had a caring daughter close by.

The notes Kerry had read mentioned another daughter. As she was nowhere to be seen, Kerry assumed they probably took shifts during the day to care for their mother.

'She's a light sleeper,' Alice said in a hushed voice. 'So she might wake up in the middle of the night. I've told her you'll be here, so it won't be a shock to see a stranger.'

'That's good, though I hope I won't be a stranger for long,' Kerry said, unable to wrench her eyes away from Alice, as though she were transfixed. 'You look exhausted. Go home and don't worry, your mum's in safe hands with me.'

An expression of relief swept over Alice's face, but her eyes were filled with sorrow as she backed away and out of the door.

Though Kerry had only been in Alice's company for a few minutes, she found herself warming to her immediately. As she watched the door close, Kerry realised she was looking forward to getting to know her better.

And of course, her mother, though the latter was an afterthought.

'So you're the nurse?' Carol suddenly said out of the blue, startling Kerry so much that she took a step back, stumbling against the wall.

'Yes.' Kerry finally found her voice. 'Nice to meet you Mrs Bridges.'

'Enough of the formalities, it's time for my medicine.' Carol pointed towards the windowsill cluttered with an array of ornaments. Kerry recognised a few of them as being collector's items. The Antiques Roadshow had been one of her favourite TV programmes at one time. Then she saw what Carol was alluding to.

Kerry looked at Carol with raised eyebrows.

'Oh don't look all self-righteous. I was on thirty a day before all this and I'm down to five now, so no nagging.'

Kerry picked up the pack of cigarettes and looked inside. There were five left of the original twenty.

Carol averted her eyes. 'Are you going to give me

one or spend all night gawping at them?'

Kerry thought for a moment, not quite sure what to do. It was Carol's house. Her lungs. But she was there to take care of her health and letting her smoke somehow didn't sit right with her. However, by the steely look in Carol's eyes she knew better than to challenge her. Not yet anyway. Once they became accustomed to one another Kerry would stamp her authority on such situations. Not only was smoking bad for Carol, but the prospect of inhaling second-hand smoke didn't exactly thrill her.

Kerry flipped a cigarette out and passed it to Carol with the lighter.

'I really don't think—' Kerry began before immediately being cut short.

'You aren't being paid to think, dear,' Carol said, luxuriantly blowing out a stream of smoke.

'I just meant—'

Carol waved away Kerry's response with a quick flick of her hand, then totally changed the subject. 'Don't suppose you'd nip downstairs and sneak up a gin and tonic, would you? Just make sure Madam Dictator doesn't get wind of it. There'll be hell to pay otherwise. For me and you.'

Kerry gulped.

What have I let myself in for? A dream job or a nightmare?

Chapter Seven

Alice smiled at her recollection of meeting Kerry earlier. She hadn't expected the agency nurse to be quite so attractive. *What was I expecting?* A woman in her sixties with a motherly bedside manner? Definitely not Kerry, that's for sure. *She's probably married with a household of kids.* Though Alice had noticed Kerry wasn't wearing a wedding ring. Not that it meant anything. Loads of married people didn't wear rings.

Letting herself into the house, Alice wasn't surprised to hear the sound of Emily tapping away on her keyboard as if she didn't have a care in the world. Why would she? Emily hadn't asked once about their mother's condition, and Alice wasn't about to update her.

Alice made her way into the kitchen in desperate need of a drink. Something to take the edge off. The shock of her mother having a stroke had knocked the stuffing out of her. Not only did it make her realise how suddenly she could have lost her, had it been more serious, but she was forced to face the reality that her mother was not immortal, and would pass away like her father. Alice would be left an orphan with only Emily as her blood relative. That thought alone gave her shivers.

Pouring wine into a glass, Alice noticed her hand tremble slightly. Stress did that to her. First the breakup with Izzy, then Carol's stroke. If things truly did happen in threes, she dreaded to think what fate had in store for her next.

'I'll have one,' Emily's voice sounded behind Alice making her jump, causing the red wine to spill over the edge of the glass and form a small puddle on the black porcelain tiled floor.

Alice immediately reached out for a paper towel to mop up the spillage, but Emily beat her to it.

'I've got it,' Emily said simply. The lack of irritation at Alice's clumsy mistake left Alice flabbergasted.

She stepped aside and watched as Emily bent over and swiftly cleaned the mess.

'Thanks.'

'Have you eaten?'

Alice frowned. Had Emily been taken over by another entity? What was her game? Not only had she spoken to Alice in the nicest way since… since well Alice couldn't remember, but she was actually acting as if she cared.

'Um, yeah, I had something round mu—earlier.' Alice reasoned it was best not to mention their mother. Not when Emily seemed in such a pleasant mood.

Emily straightened and poured herself a drink. She stared at Alice as if she wanted to say something but changed her mind. Without saying another word, she brushed past Alice and left the kitchen.

Alice stared at the kitchen door long and hard until her vision became blurred. *What the fuck! What the hell is her problem?*

It was bad enough that she'd had to put up with

Carol sniping at her all day, the last thing she needed to deal with was Emily's hostile attitude. Surely Emily understood the pressure Alice was under. Dealing with their mother was a pain at the best of times, but now Carol had lost her independence, it was infinitely worse. Alice prayed the doctor was right about the swift recovery.

Grabbing the bottle of wine by the neck, Alice took it with her to her bedroom. She was angry with herself for thinking that Carol would change, and that Emily had somehow mellowed in the space of a couple of days.

As much as Alice hated to admit it, she realised that it was too late for either of them to have a transformation. Carol didn't even think she had a problem, and Emily's hatred and resentment targeted at anyone she was related to seemed to have seeped inside her veins.

Sitting on the edge of the bed, Alice came to another realisation. She didn't need Emily's help. Not now that Kerry was caring for their mother.

Although Alice felt guilty for foisting Carol's care onto someone else, Alice had so far managed to convince herself that she had done the right thing. As much as she loved her, Alice knew looking after Carol seven days a week would have been counterproductive. She would never have been able to do anything right as far as Carol was concerned which would have only caused her more stress.

Alice only hoped that Carol wouldn't give Kerry a

hard time. It was one thing for Carol to make Alice feel less than she was, but quite another to do it to a complete stranger.

Alice knew Kerry would be able to handle her, seeing as nurses and doctors dealt with stubborn, rude, obnoxious patients all the time. Hospitals didn't have posters warning of a zero-tolerance policy for any kind of abuse levelled at staff for no reason.

Not that Alice could imagine anyone being disrespectful to Kerry. The moment their eyes met, Alice saw the compassion only someone comfortable walking in other's pain could have.

Alice liked Kerry immediately, and she couldn't help but wonder what kind of person Kerry was outside her role. Was she as kind and gentle as she seemed? *She must be.* You couldn't switch kindness on and off, and from what Alice had seen of Kerry so far, she seemed genuine. Something that was becoming more of a rarity in life.

Alice didn't know if it was down to people becoming more insular because of technology, where they could present a different version of themselves to the world, but trying to connect with people was proving harder than ever. Especially when it came to her sister.

Aren't twins meant to be inseparable? Alice snorted. *Whoever came up with that idea obviously didn't have a twin themselves.*

Alice drained her glass and refilled it. *I should never have come here! Why did I think things would be any different?*

And now she was stuck. For the time being

anyway. As soon as her mum was back on her feet, Alice would be on the first plane out of Heathrow airport and she would not look back.

I've just got to bide my time until then… and more importantly, stay the hell out of Emily's way.

Letting out a long yawn, Alice placed the glass on the bedside cabinet, undressed and slipped under the goose down quilt, pulling it tight around her body.

When she finally fell asleep, she was beset with dreams of her mother calling out for her help. Carol needed her, but Alice couldn't reach her no matter how hard she tried. Waking with a start, her heart pounded hard against her chest, endless tears streaming down her cheeks. Wiping them away roughly with the back of her hand, Alice put in a quick call to Kerry and her reassurance immediately allayed her fears. Kerry informed her that Carol had slept peacefully throughout the night, had willingly taken her medication and was now tucking into scrambled eggs and smoked salmon. Alice laughed when she heard this. That was typically how their relationship went. Alice was always in a constant panic about her mother's welfare, while Carol carried on with her day-to-day life oblivious.

Thinking about it as she often did, Alice knew the blurred mother-daughter boundary between them was no one's fault but her own. Her mother took everything she could from Alice and Alice gave everything she had, having been trained from an early age to put her mother's feelings above her own. Even at thirty-four and being somewhat conscious of the unhealthy dynamic between them, Alice still didn't have the tools to untangle the mesh which ensnared her.

An hour later, Alice was dressed, and like the dutiful daughter she was, ready to make her way over to her mother's to relieve Kerry.

She thought about leaving Emily a note, informing her that she'd be back late that evening, but decided against it. It wasn't as if Emily even cared whether or not Alice returned anyway. She'd probably be relieved if Alice stayed with their mum indefinitely. That option had fleetingly crossed Alice's mind when she left Izzy's, but her body physically recoiled at the suggestion.

Closing the front door behind her as quietly as she could, Alice had a spring in her step as she made her way down the path and to her car. She was very much looking forward to seeing Kerry again. Even if it was only for a few minutes.

The early morning sky was cloudless, and the smell of spring was in the air. Both were a welcome relief from the miserable weather they'd endured up until recently. There was nothing worse than being unhappy and stuck indoors while it rained outside.

Arriving at her mother's house shortly after, Alice walked straight around the back, knowing that her mum would doubtless be on the decking on such a nice day.

Carol's 'happy place' as she called it. Surprisingly, the garden was the only space that was spared clutter of any kind. The luscious green lawn was mowed once a week by a local teenager Carol never interacted with, she merely left his payment of £15 under a stone near the wooden hut at the back. Long stemmed roses swayed gently from side to side in the warm breeze, and the assortment of colourful flowers Alice had seeded months earlier now blossomed under the warmth of the sun's rays.

Alice rounded the corner and ducked under the overgrown archway, slowing upon hearing two voices giggling.

Entering by the side gate, she spotted her mum first, sat at the wooden garden table in a wheelchair, puffing merrily away on a cigarette. Ellen, her mum's best friend, sat opposite, elegantly wafting aside the second-hand smoke heading her way.

Alice was disappointed not to see Kerry at the table with them, but her dismay was short lived. By the time she'd locked the gate behind her, Kerry stepped out from the kitchen carrying a silver tray on which sat two long slimline glasses, each with a blue straw bobbling in the liquid.

Alice's mood brightened immediately as they exchanged a smile. Kerry had changed from the nurse's uniform she'd worn the previous night. Today, she wore a yellow shirt, a pair of black cropped jeans and black sandals. Her thick straight hair hung carelessly over her shoulders.

'Alice, there you are. Carol told me you were coming by today. I haven't seen you in an age,' Ellen said, removing an extremely large pair of sunglasses that almost covered her petite face.

Alice wandered over to Ellen and bent down to

hug her. 'I know, what's it been? Like six months?'

'More like a year, but who's counting.' Ellen laughed, running her hand over the top of her short silver hair. 'You're looking well.'

'Thanks. You too.' And she did. Ellen didn't look a day over fifty despite being in her late sixties. She said her secret to a youthful appearance was plenty of sex and a stress-free life. Carol had thought her comment distasteful at the time, but Alice couldn't think of a better mindset to have.

'And you're still with…' Ellen paused as she grappled for the right name, the sun glinting off the large diamond ring on her wedding finger. 'Isabel?'

Alice didn't care to correct her, instead she smiled sweetly. 'She's fine. How's Paul?'

Ellen rolled her eyes. 'The same. Attached to his mobile phone and Twitter.'

Alice turned to her mother as Carol held a tall glass of clear, fizzy liquid to her mouth. *Gin and tonic at this time of the morning. Kerry should know better.*

As if reading her mind, Kerry shook her head as a wide smile curved her lips, 'It's sparkling water with a twist of lemon.'

The heat crept up Alice's neck. *What was I thinking? As if a nurse would give her patient alcohol first thing in the morning.*

'The cigarettes I can't control, I'm afraid,' Kerry said as a plume of smoke filled the space between them.

'Don't worry, not even God himself could get her to quit.'

'Do you two mind? I'm sitting here you know.' Carol snorted. 'Discussing me like I'm invisible.'

'Nobody could miss you, Mum,' Alice said lightly, not wanting Carol to kick off in front of Kerry. Not for her own sake but to ensure Kerry didn't leave after her first shift having re-thought her position.

Any kind of help Alice hired for her mother over the years hadn't lasted long. Only Bill, the handy man, had managed to endure six months of employment, but Alice knew it was only because he turned his hearing aid off as soon as he arrived.

'Sarcasm doesn't become you dear,' Carol said, glaring at Alice as if she wished she could make her disappear from view.

Alice knew better than to react to Carol's words, as an argument would ensue, and the silent treatment would follow for God knows how many hours or even days.

Kerry gave Alice a sympathetic glance before bending over to pick up her bag.

'Right, I'd better be off.' Kerry looked down at Carol. 'I'll see you tonight?'

'Well, I'm hardly going anywhere, am I?' Carol crushed her cigarette in the ashtray and immediately lit another.

'It was lovely to meet you, Ellen,' Kerry said with a warm smile.

Alice suppressed a smile at the way Kerry ignored Carol's passive-aggressive comment. As much as she'd tried over the years to do the same, Alice still hadn't managed to grasp that 'don't give a fuck attitude', mainly because Alice did care. *Too much.*

Kerry turned and walked towards Alice. 'Good to see you again.'

Just five simple words from Kerry's mouth were enough to make Alice's dread of a whole day with her mother simply fade away.

'You too,' Alice said.

Alice met her gaze, a fiery recognition evident in Kerry's eyes.

Kerry stood opposite longer than necessary then, as if coming to her senses, she gave a quick wave and walked briskly around to the exit.

Alice sat down at the table, butterflies dancing in her stomach at the unexpected encounter.

'So, what d'you think?' Carol asked.

'About what?' Alice asked, trying to play it cool, her face still flushed.

'About Kerry. Who d'you think I'm talking about? The man down the road?'

Alice suppressed a sigh. 'She seems nice.'

'Yes, I thought you'd like her.' Carol's eyes narrowed. 'You're more like your father than I realised.'

The comment was intentionally spiteful, but Alice smiled anyway. She wasn't going to let her mother get her down when this was the happiest she'd felt in a long time.

'I thought she was very nice too,' Ellen quickly interjected.

Alice couldn't fail to notice the knowing expression

on Ellen's face. Did she realise Alice found Kerry attractive? She'd never been able to get away with lying to Ellen, even as a kid. Her inquisitive gaze always gave the impression she could see right into Alice's soul. Which in turn caused Alice to descend into a gibbering wreck, spilling the beans on whatever mischief she and Emily had got up to.

'I suppose the proof will be what she's like with you, Mum,' Alice said in an attempt to direct the conversation to neutral ground.

'I wish my daughter was as caring as you, Alice,' Ellen said. 'I know you worry a lot about your mum—'

'Worry! That one?' Carol barely looked at Alice. 'She'd have had me put in a home if my stroke would've been serious. And after all the things I've done for my kids.'

'Come on, Carol, you know that's not true.'

'She said so herself, ask her, go on.'

Alice wanted the ground to swallow her whole. What had been an absent-minded remark said to her mother a week earlier, had obviously been taken to heart.

'Mum, you're taking things out of context, I didn't mean it like that.'

This was Alice's way of saying that yes, her mother was right in one sense, in that she may have been a tad insensitive, but there had been some truth in her comment. One of the nurses had told Alice that family members are ill equipped to care for serious stroke victims which was true. As such, Alice had innocently relayed the comment to her mother by saying, 'It's a good thing your stroke wasn't serious otherwise you might have needed twenty-four-hour care'.

'Well, if you think that's bad, you should hear what my Jill says to me.' Ellen laughed, making light of the situation. 'She's always telling me she's going to put me in home the first sign of being forgetful.'

'The difference is Jill's a good girl.' Carol paused for a moment then continued in her 'woe is me voice' – a well-worn instrument used to secure sympathy. 'She loves you. I honestly don't know what I did to deserve a daughter like her, I really don't.'

Carol turned and glared at Alice, her deep-set wrinkles forming a scowl, remnants of spittle gathering at the corners of her mouth.

The truth eluded Carol. Every word expelled from her mouth only served to further her own reality, regardless of its relation to the real world. It didn't occur to Carol that what she said was absolute nonsense and at best, a pack of lies, but it never did.

There was no point challenging her.

Content she'd painted Alice in the worst possible light, Carol triumphantly slipped another cigarette between her lips. As she lifted the lighter to her face, she missed the touching moment Ellen patted Alice's leg under the table and the look of sympathy in her eyes.

Why was it that everyone saw how Carol's behaviour affected Alice except Carol herself?

Chapter Eight

Harry's café was nestled amongst a row of independent shops only ten minutes from Kerry's flat, so when Debbie called her en-route home and asked if she wanted to meet there for breakfast, Kerry jumped at the chance. Although she'd barely slept in twenty-four hours, Kerry knew if she went to bed now, she'd spend the next few hours tossing and turning.

Best to eat first and wind down for a bit.

The aroma of bacon greeted Kerry's nostrils as soon as she pushed the rustic wooden framed glass door open and stepped into the café. Though the premises were fairly small, only having enough room for seven square tables covered with plastic red and white checkered tablecloths, the café was always busy.

On hearing the bell above the door sound, Harry, a barrel-chested man in his late sixties with silver-streaked hair, looked up from the sizzling grill he stood over and wiped his hands across his pristine white apron.

He gave Kerry a bright smile and called out over the loud chatter of diners in his thick Yorkshire accent. 'Usual love?'

Kerry returned the smile and nodded. A bacon sandwich on brown bread and a cup of tea. The duo always went down a treat.

Spotting Debbie near the back, Kerry walked over

to her, kissing her cheek before sinking down into a chair opposite.

'You, my dear, look exhausted.'

'And you, my dear, would be right in your assumption,' Kerry replied, slipping her aching feet out of her sandals, and resting them on top.

'How did last night go?' Debbie asked, taking a mouthful of tea.

'Well,' Kerry said frowning. 'I think it did anyway.'

Debbie's eyebrows rose, while giving Kerry a questioning look. 'Meaning?'

'Meaning… Oh thank you,' Kerry said to the waitress who plonked a mug of tea down in front of her. 'Meaning I don't really know. The client seems a bit of an odd ball.'

'In what way?'

'I dunno. She's nice enough, bit domineering, which is fine in itself. Who wants a stranger in their house when they're at their most vulnerable, right? But it's the way she treats her daughter…'

Debbie wiggled her eyebrows. 'She has a daughter, eh? Now this is interestin'.'

'Don't start getting ideas, it's not like that,' Kerry said, blowing on the surface of her tea.

Even as the words left her mouth, Kerry questioned her response. She couldn't deny being drawn to Alice, and why should she? It was natural to find someone attractive. But if so, why did she feel so guilty about it? And more importantly, why couldn't she bring herself to tell Debbie?

Because she'll make a mountain out of a molehill, that's why!

'Go on then. Tell me about the daughter…'

'Well, she seems really nice and obviously cares very much about her mum, but the way she treats her is almost like she doesn't really like her…'

'I'm confused, who? The mother or the daughter?'

'The mother, she treats her daughter as if she's an afterthought.' Kerry took a sip of her tea. 'Sorry, I'm not making any sense but it's like watching a child try to get their mother's attention only to be rejected.'

Suddenly remembering the hurt and vulnerable look on Alice's face, Kerry decided not to elaborate further. She didn't want to betray Alice's trust even though she barely knew the woman.

In that moment, when Carol had been so dismissive, she'd wanted to gather Alice in her arms and protect her. Or better still, get her the hell away from Carol. She'd had to remind herself that she was their employee, no more, no less, and it was not her place to get involved in their personal affairs, but it had been hard.

'Is that it?' Debbie asked, raising her eyebrows.

Kerry knew Debbie wanted to hear something more salacious, of how they'd slipped into the spare room and shagged the night away. *I wish.*

She felt a bit silly now blowing a small incident out of proportion, but her gut instinct told her Carol's treatment towards Alice which might not seem a big deal to an outsider looking in, was probably a big issue for Alice.

The waitress brought Kerry's sandwich over and she took a bite before the plate even reached the table. She ate in silence for a few minutes, aware Debbie was eyeing her suspiciously.

'What?' Kerry said once her mouth was empty.

'How old's the daughter?'

Kerry shrugged. 'Around the same age as me. Why?'

'So she's a big girl who can speak up for herself. Don't start lookin' at her like one of your pet projects that needs savin'.'

'I didn't say she needs saving. I just felt sorry for her that's all.'

''Cause her mum bitched at her? Go into any house across the country and I'm sure you'll hear a lot worse.'

Kerry thought about it for a few moments. As always, Debbie made a valid point. She was overthinking. The lack of sleep wasn't helping either.

Debbie ordered another cup of tea for them both.

'So,' Debbie said, leaning forward. 'Is she hot?'

'Who?'

'The daughter?'

Kerry's stomach constricted at the thought of Alice. 'She's all right.'

'Just all right?' Debbie asked with a wink.

A rush of heat rose to Kerry's face. 'Yes, Debs, just all right.'

Debbie grinned. 'OK but if you want my advice,

I'd leave it well alone.'

'I haven't—'

'I know you haven't done anythin', Kerry, but I know you. Once you start gettin' into that maternal place with someone, you can't hold back. This is a short-term job by the sounds of it, so don't start gettin' emotionally involved up here.' Debbie tapped her temples. 'It'll all end in tears, trust me.'

'I totally agree but nothing's going to happen.'

'And you're sure you want it to stay that way?'

Kerry nodded. *And even if I didn't, I wouldn't tell you. I can't even admit how I feel to myself.*

Chapter Nine

If Alice had ever been more grateful for an ally, it was now. Ellen called her husband to let him know she would be staying at Carol's place until Kerry started her shift that night. This meant Alice could escape early, even if by a few hours.

Arriving back at Emily's, she'd spent the evening alone with nothing but a notebook and pen. It was hard for her to write her feelings down on the page. Every time she tried, tears prickled the back of her eyes causing her to stop. It was as if by writing the words down, they were actually true. Her mother hated her. Or if it wasn't that drastic, at least resented being her mother. How else could Alice explain the way she treated her? How little she thought of her as her own flesh and blood.

Alice knew if she didn't put her foot down, it would never end. Though she had discussed things with Emily in the past and they'd both deemed the situation unbearable, both had little faith things would ever change. That's why Emily had made the break. Alice always thought she took the easy way out. It was Alice who should have cut ties with her first. After all, she was the one being mistreated.

She checked her phone – 2 a.m. Alice hadn't realised how quickly the time had flown by. Looking down at the paper, all that remained were several sentences scribbled out. Eventually, she realised there was no point in trying to confront her mother. Not yet anyway.

Hours later, barely having had any sleep, Alice was again making the journey she had now grown to hate. Once in a while hadn't been too bad but driving to see her mother every day was a new kind of torture. Well not completely. *There's one light at the end of the tunnel.* Her lips curved into a smile. *Kerry.*

'I'm so sorry I'm late.' Alice burst into the kitchen as if the house was on fire. Her usual twenty-minute journey had taken her nearly an hour and a half. 'There was a massive traffic jam and—'

Kerry held up her hand and smiled. 'It's fine, honestly. I'm not in any rush.'

Alice slipped out of her jacket and hung it on the back of her chair. Sensing something was different in her immediate surroundings, it only took a few seconds to realise what it was. Scanning the room in amazement, she was speechless. The once cluttered kitchen was now orderly and neat, every plate and cup exactly where it should be. Old newspapers were stuffed in a makeshift recycling bag by the door, and she could actually see the surface of the worktop – something that hadn't been visible for years.

Alice gave a slow nod in appreciation. 'Florence Nightingale and super cleaner all in one? Very impressive. You'll have to stay for a coffee. It's the least I can offer for what you've done.'

'Sounds good to me,' Kerry said, sitting at the dining table. 'And don't worry about the cleaning. I'd rather be doing something than sitting around bored. Mary's been with your mum for the last hour.'

Kerry's agreement to stay lightened Alice's spirits. There was no denying she enjoyed Kerry being in the house. She radiated a warmth that comforted Alice, as if wrapping her safely in a cocoon.

'Milk? Sugar?' Alice asked, thinking how weird it felt making coffee for Kerry in her mum's kitchen. Just a few days ago, she didn't know the woman existed. Now it was as if Kerry had always been a part of her life.

'Just milk please,' Kerry said.

Alice spoke as she walked around, taking the coffee out of the cupboard and spooning it into two mugs. She wanted to know everything there was to know about Kerry.

'So how long have you been a nurse?'

'Twelve years.'

'That's some commitment, I take it you like it?' Alice said in an attempt to keep the conversation flowing.

Kerry leant back in her chair. 'I'd go one step further than that and say I love it.'

Alice turned away from the worktop to face her. 'I'm glad. It's so fulfilling doing a job you actually enjoy.'

'What do you do?'

'I'm a…' Alice caught herself. She wasn't anything now apart from unemployed. 'Sorry, was a financial trader.'

'Wow, that must take nerves of steel, dealing with vast sums of money.'

'Not really.' Alice turned back to the job at hand. She'd be lying if she said she hadn't been overwhelmed at the start, but over time she had become desensitised and didn't really give much thought to how much she was risking. All she'd cared about was being successful.

'You say that so casually.' Kerry laughed.

Her soft laughter was the nicest sound Alice had heard in a long while.

'They're just numbers on a screen,' Alice said. 'It would be different if we dealt in hard currency. Now that would be scary.'

'I suppose… You said you *were* a trader?'

'Yeah, I got fired,' Alice said matter-of-factly. She said it with such ease and no shame she shocked herself. To admit her failure to Izzy would have been unthinkable, but with Kerry, it was if Alice instinctively knew she wouldn't judge her. 'Whatever you do, don't tell my mum.'

Kerry zipped her lips closed with her fingers. 'Not a word. Your secret is safe with me.'

'Thanks.'

Alice placed a mug on a rattan coaster in front of Kerry, one she hadn't seen since 1995.

'Where did you find these?' Alice said, lowering herself onto the wooden dining room chair.

'I rearranged one of the cupboards, I found some matching place mats too.' Kerry took a sip of her coffee and sighed. 'I needed this, thanks.'

'You're welcome.'

Alice surveyed the room, unable to believe the

difference.

'You must be wondering why I haven't sorted this place out myself.'

Kerry frowned. 'No, not at all. It's your mum's house after all, I'm sure you have enough on your plate.'

Alice stared at her mug, tracing the outline of the cartoon cat with her fingernail. 'She's a difficult woman, and a hoarder. If I'd have done this,' Alice said, gesturing to her surroundings with a wave of her hand, 'she would've lost the plot. When she knows this is down to you, she'll just use it as another stick to beat me with. She'll tell me how wonderful you are and what a horrible daughter I am for not doing it.'

'Oh no, I'm so sorry! I shouldn't have touched anything.'

'Don't be silly, I'm really glad you did. Something has to give, she can't carry on living like this.'

Alice glanced at Kerry's lips, her mind suddenly changing track and going off on its own tangent as she imagined what they would feel like pressed against her own, what her kiss would taste like.

'So, are you looking for work in the same area?' Kerry said, staring straight into Alice's eyes. If Kerry noticed the desire in them, she didn't let on.

Alice shook her head. 'To be honest, I don't know what I want to do at the moment. I'm just taking one day at a time. Unfortunately, I found out the hard way that planning for the future is a mug's game.'

'You think?'

'Most definitely.'

They drank in silence until Kerry spoke again.

'Your mum had a peaceful night.'

Alice lowered her eyes to her cup. 'Good.'

'About yesterday—'

'Are you the only nurse in your family?' Alice said, deliberately cutting her off. She knew what Kerry was going to say but didn't want to hear it, because if she did, Alice would have to justify her mother's behaviour yet again.

Alice looked up from her cup and found Kerry staring directly at her again. A look so intense Alice had to restrain herself from covering her eyes with her hands. She felt like a schoolgirl with her first crush. *Jesus, that's what it is!* She realised with a start.

'No, just me, my mum was a pilot, and my dad's in IT,' Kerry finally said, breaking her gaze. 'I read in your notes that you have a sister.'

'Yeah.' Alice stood and took her cup to the sink.

'Will she be coming over at any point? I thought it would be nice to meet the whole family—'

'That won't be happening any time soon,' Alice said abruptly.

'Oh right.'

Alice poured the contents of her cup down the drain.

'I'm sorry if I got too personal,' Kerry said, her hair falling gently to her shoulders in waves as she removed her hair band.

Alice looked at her. Her anger quickly fading and giving way to something softer. 'You didn't. It's just that my sister is the last person I want to talk about at the moment.'

'I understand. Tensions often run high in stressful situations like this.'

'Things went off track with Emily way before my mum's stroke,'

Just then Carols voice sounded down the hallway. 'Alice is that you?

'Yes mum, won't be a minute,' Alice called out as she moved towards the door. Then she said to Kerry, 'I'd better let you get on. You must be tired.'

Kerry glanced down at her still half-full cup but remained silent. She stood and grabbed her jacket from the back of the chair before checking through her bag.

Alice gestured for Kerry to lead the way and followed her along the hallway to the front door. As hard as Alice tried not to, she noticed the rhythmic sway of Kerry's hips and the shapely way she filled out the jeans she was wearing. The sight was hypnotic.

Stop behaving like a teenager and be professional!

'Is everything OK?' Kerry said as they reached the door.

The hallway was narrow, too narrow for two people to remain far apart from one another. The scent of her perfume wasn't helping matters.

'Yes, I'm fine,' Alice said, thinking how much she wanted to kiss Kerry. The close proximity was pure torture.

Kerry opened the door and stepped out through the threshold.

'Well, I guess I'll see you soon,' Alice said, glad Kerry was out of reach.

'For sure.' Kerry hurried down the pathway, calling back over her shoulder. 'Have a good day.'

Alice closed the door, leant back against it and smiled to herself.

Chapter Ten

Completing the chapter on 'Clyde, the family man' was hard for Emily. This should have been a time to thrust the light on her father's warm and loving nature towards his wife and children, instead, the page spewed hate and bitterness, and rightly so. By the time she'd written the final word, memories buried so deep she forgot they existed, resurfaced, bringing with them a whole new slew of emotions.

Emily could have summed up the chapter in a few words. Clyde was a weak man. The sort of person who ran away from his responsibilities when the going got tough. Someone who abandoned his wife and children for a younger woman.

And look where that got him, dying alone with no one by his side to whisper words of comfort as he took his last breath.

What shook Emily was how blind Alice was to their father's flaws. He hadn't tried to reach out to them until they were eighteen, a time when they were deemed adults and didn't need looking after. Emily still held a modicum of hope that once she'd read the complete book, she would understand why Emily was determined to shed light on their childhood and the emotional damage caused by his abandonment. There was hope. After all, they once shared the same values, the same everything really.

Their mother on the other hand, Emily could not

forgive for the blatant disregard of care during their childhood.

The doorbell rang catching Emily by surprise. She wasn't expecting anyone.

Assuming Alice had probably lost her key, she jumped up to let her in.

Pulling back the door, Emily turned without uttering a word and strode back towards her office. It was only hearing a male voice that stopped her abruptly in her tracks.

'Emily…'

He sounded familiar. A voice Emily hadn't heard in years but one she would never forget.

Turning slowly, her eyes widened at the sight of the man she once loved as a father – Arnold. Her father's best friend.

The once strong and vibrant man Emily remembered was now frail, leaning unsteadily on the walking stick he held by his side.

'Arnold?' Emily said weakly, the words forming more of a question than a statement.

'The one and only,' Arnold said, smiling. His once thick curly black hair was now fully grey. His eyes sunken, his cheeks sullen.

Emily rushed forward and embraced him, holding on as if he'd been resurrected from the dead. The familiar musty cigar scent evoking childhood nostalgia.

Placing his arm around her, Arnold patted her back reassuringly.

'Can I come in?' Arnold said, shifting his weight

from one foot to the other. 'I can't stand for long.'

Emily drew back. 'I'm sorry, of course.'

'Nothing to be sorry for,' Arnold said smiling as he took her arm and let her lead him into the living room.

Once seated on the sofa beside Emily, he took her hands in his own.

'Life seems to be treating you well,' Arnold said, taking in the tastefully decorated room.

'I've no complaints,' Emily replied. 'How are you?'

'Old. You never think it's going to happen to you then one day you wake up and realise you're living with one foot in the grave,' he said with humour.

'It is so good to see you. I've often thought about you…'

'And here I am.'

'Yes, here you are,' Emily said squeezing his bony, wrinkled hands. 'So what brings you here?'

Arnold lowered his gaze briefly. 'I heard you're writing Clyde's biography.'

Emily dropped his hands and got to her feet. Even in his death, her father still had his protectors.

'How? Only a few people know.'

'People talk in the industry, Em.'

Emily just hoped her mother hadn't caught wind of what she was doing. She could only imagine what she'd have to say about it.

'OK, so what if I am? What's it got to do with you?'

Emily's demeanour was no longer admiring, she

was in defensive mode. Combative. Ready to take on anyone that tried to distort the reality of what she knew to be true deep in her heart.

'I want to set the record straight about a few things before you make the biggest mistake of your life.'

'Then you've wasted your precious time. I know the truth about my father.'

Arnold struggled to his feet, waving away her offer of help.

'Emily, there's more to this story than you know. No doubt your mum's told you her side, which has influenced your version, and there's the truth. The question is, do you want to hear it?'

Chapter Eleven

Considering 'Closing down' sale signs screamed at customers from the window outside, Plunder, was relatively empty – the discounts obviously not enough to entice passing trade. Not that Alice was surprised. Most of the clothes in stock would only fit women built like a stick.

'I'm sorry, Alice, but Izzy is a class A bitch!' Stella, Alice's best friend since childhood, leant forward. 'And if I'm being honest, I never really liked her. There was something shifty about her.'

'And you're telling me this now?' Alice asked, raising her eyebrows at a top she wouldn't have been able to fit her hand in let alone anything else.

'Well, I wasn't going to say anything while you were dating her, was I? That's not what friends do.'

'You mean it's OK for friends to lie?' Alice said. She put the top back on a pile of others that had carelessly been discarded.

'Of course not, but not saying anything isn't exactly a lie.'

Alice raised her hands. 'OK, let's just leave it at that, shall we? I have more important things to be worrying about.'

At least Alice should have, but thoughts of Kerry filled her mind. It was an odd situation to find herself in. She split up with Izzy after two years and felt… nothing. Zilch. As if their relationship hadn't taken place at all. Now her mind was occupied with a stranger she'd only met a few days ago. What was that about? How could she have moved on in her mind so quickly? Alice had to question whether she really loved Izzy at all if this was the case.

Stella picked up a shirt from the clothes rail and eyed it with disdain. 'Is this what passes for fashion these days?'

Alice looked at the skimpy leopard skin print and laughed. 'Apparently it does.'

'Disgusting. Might as well not wear anything at all.'

'That's coming from you,' Alice said, still in the throes of laughter. 'How many times did your dad ground you for wearing next to nothing on a night out?'

'Things were different back then,' Stella said defensively before bursting out into laughter herself. 'The shit I put my poor dad through, I'm surprised he didn't have a heart attack.'

'Yet look at you now, Ms Respectability herself.'

'I don't know about that.' Stella giggled as she grabbed Alice by the arm. 'I know it's early but I'm gagging for a drink.'

'OK but I can't drink, I told my mum we were going shopping. I don't think she'd be too impressed if I go back stinking like a brewery.'

'Fine. I'll drink for two.'

'Come on then.'

Alice let herself be dragged out onto the concourse and up to the next level where a pub was situated. It was mostly empty except for a couple at the bar ordering drinks. The barman took their order and within minutes placed a bottle of wine in a silver bucket in front of Stella, advising them that a waiter would bring Alice's coffee over to her.

Once seated, Stella took a long sip of her chardonnay, then relaxed back in her seat.

'I needed that.'

'What's up with you anyway? You looked more stressed than I feel.'

'Life.'

Alice smiled at the waiter when he placed her coffee in front of her. 'As in…?'

'As in everything.' Stella's light-hearted persona quickly vanished as a dark expression suddenly clouded her face. 'I'm just pissed off with it all. It's like Groundhog Day. Everything's the same. Nothing changes… I might as well be dead.'

Surprised by her sudden mood change, Alice said, 'That's a bit dramatic, isn't it?'

'Not really.' Stella shrugged. 'I mean, if I died tomorrow, what the hell would I miss? It just all seems so pointless.'

'What's started all this then?'

'Everything and nothing.'

'Why don't I believe you?' Alice said, wondering if this had to do with Stella's job as a therapist. This wasn't the first time Stella had suffered burn out from the endless hours she worked. Listening to client's problems all day would overwhelm even the most resilient of people.

'OK, so if you really want to know the truth, here it is… When you told me about your mum's stroke, I had a bit of an epiphany. I took a long hard look at my life and realised… I've wasted it.'

Alice reached across the table and took hold of Stella's hand. To look at her, Stella had everything anyone could ever want. Good looks, a good job, a husband that adored her and a child Stella loved more than life itself.

'Are you joking? You've led an amazing life, look at—'

'Yes, look at all the material things I have, but that's all.'

'But what about Fred, and Timmy?'

Stella avoided eye contact. 'It's complicated.'

'Ah the good ole "it's complicated" blocker to avoid just saying what it is.'

'If you really want to know… I love Fred… but I'm not in love with him. To be honest, I don't think I ever was.'

'Is there someone else?'

Stella snorted. 'I wish.'

Alice couldn't help but feel some responsibility for the sudden car crash in Stella's life. If she'd known Stella would have had this kind of reaction to the news of her mum's incident, she'd have kept her mouth shut.

'So, what're you going to do?'

'Nothing. Just live the rest of my life in misery. And I know I should know better than to give in to my emotions, but sometimes you just reach the end of the rope and wonder if there's any point in holding on.' Stella cast her eyes down at her glass. 'That's why I've always envied you…'

'Me?' Alice said, her eyeballs nearly popping out of their sockets at the very thought.

'Yeah, even though it was tough for you coming out, you just did it. You didn't care about the obstacles in front of you.'

'That's different. I didn't have a choice.'

'Yes, you did, you could've chosen to lie to yourself like the millions of closeted people out there. You could've led a double life, smiling to the outside world while crawling on your knees in private.'

'Is that how you feel?'

Stella slowly nodded, tears brimming in her eyes. Each word leaving her mouth seemed to do so under duress. 'Every day's a struggle, Al.'

Alice's throat tightened. 'Why haven't you told me this before?'

'Because I didn't want to burden you with my problems.'

Blinking away the tears welling in her own eyes, Alice dug into her bag and took out her phone. Quickly tapping in a message, she waited a few seconds for the response, before putting the phone back in her bag. Pushing her coffee aside, she reached over for the empty glass and filled it with wine.

'Right, Ellen's going to stay with my mum until her nurse arrives. Now, it's time for me and you to have a serious talk.'

***

One bottle of wine had soon turned into three. There had been many tears and lots of laughter as Alice encouraged Stella to release all her emotions. Four hours later, though very drunk, Stella appeared in much brighter spirits and Alice sat in the back of a cab desperate for the toilet.

Why didn't I go before I left?

With another thirty minutes of the journey remaining, Alice didn't think she'd make it in time. Peering out through the window, a thought came to her as they passed a row of familiar shops.

'Could you drop me somewhere else instead please? Just take the next right.'

'Sure,' the driver replied, a scrawny man whose greasy hair hung limp around his shoulders.

Alice already had the door open ready to jump out before the cab came to a standstill outside her mother's house.

'Thanks,' she said, handing him some cash as she leapt from the car and sprinted up the path.

Fumbling to get her keys in the lock, she eventually burst into the hallway, colliding with Kerry. Alice grabbed her, pulling Kerry tight against her to stop her falling backwards and, for a moment, they stood as one, silently staring into each other's eyes, until Alice's bladder sent an emergency call to her brain.

'Sorry, I need to pee… bad!' Alice said, stepping

back and giving Kerry the once over to make sure she was OK before darting up the stairs to the toilet.

Moments later, as Alice washed her hands, she stared at her reflection in the mirror. Her cheeks were flushed, more to do with her thoughts about Kerry than the alcohol she realised. The heat from Kerry's body being so close only minutes earlier had ignited all her senses.

I've only just broken up with Izzy. Now is not the time to obsess over some other woman I barely know.

No matter how many times Alice told herself she was being stupid, she just couldn't get Kerry out of her mind. Half the time Alice didn't even know what she was thinking about, but she just knew her presence was there. Like a shadow in the darkness.

'Is that you Alice?' Carol's voice sounded from the room next door.

Damn! Alice had hoped to pop in for the loo then leave straight away. *No such luck.* The woman had the hearing of an owl.

Alice set off to her mother's bedroom. Tapping gently on the door, she pushed it open upon hearing her mum call out to enter.

Propped up against two pillows, Carol eyed her with disgust when Alice sat on the end of the bed.

'It's all right for some, isn't it?'

Alice took the rebuke in silence, hesitating before answering moments later. 'Aren't I allowed to go out and enjoy myself occasionally?'

'Of course you are,' Carol said, her voice lacking

sincerity. 'What do you care that I'm stuck in this room suffering?'

'You're hardly suffering, Mum.' She was doing it again. Trying to make her feel guilty for having a life. A tactic she'd used since Alice was a teenager.

'What do you know?' Carol demanded in an imperious tone.

Unwilling to be drawn into an argument, Alice placated her instead. 'You're right, I don't know… I'm sorry… is there anything I can do for you?'

Carol ignored her question. 'What're you doing here at this time of night, drunk at that?'

'I was at a bar with Stella and I needed to use the toilet.'

'Stella. Is she still the local bike?' Carol said, shaking her head in disgust. 'That woman should be the one in the patient's chair not the one giving advice. She's a disgrace.'

Her mother couldn't let go of the wild image she had of Stella growing up.

'I'm sure a lot of her clients would disagree,' Alice said in Stella's defence.

Carol ignored Alice's input and continued her tirade. 'The stress that woman must have put her poor mother through. She nearly had it as bad as me, having to put up with you. At least she didn't have the police turning up, and the shame of her neighbours gossiping about her.'

Oh God, here we go again!

The incident Carol was referring to must have

taken place at least twenty years previously. Carol's version of events involved Alice trashing the house and causing Carol a major embarrassment when the police turned up about the noise disturbance coming from Alice's bedroom.

The actual truth? Their neighbour at the time, Blythe, had called the police because she thought someone was trying to break into her house. The police had popped next door to ask if anyone in the household had seen anything. It was when one of the police officers saw the state of their house and remarked that it looked like the place had been ransacked, Carol had been horrified by his reaction and re-wrote the story in her head so she could project her shame. Alice being Alice never took the time to correct Carol on what had really taken place.

Over the years, Carol had accepted her own version of events as the truth. Apparently, just thinking about the incident still caused Carol to suffer intense stress, often equating it to having PTSD. Sometimes, just sometimes, Alice tried to understand why their father hadn't left years before he did.

'Now Izzy, I bet her mother's proud of her?' Carol said, suddenly out of the blue.

'Izzy?' Alice asked, trying to play it cool. Had she called her? Did her mother know they'd broken up? Is that why she was being so mean?

'Yes Izzy. I don't know what that woman sees in you. I really don't,' Carol said. 'And then there're are some people have the worst luck.'

'Who're we talking about now?' Alice asked at the sudden change in conversation. Her mother did that sometimes, she'd be talking about one thing then without any warning, start on another topic and get angry with Alice when she couldn't keep up.

'Kerry and her girlfriend. Don't suppose she'll ever get over it. I mean, you only have one true love, don't you agree?'

Kerry is gay! That thought quickly dissolved as the rest of her mum's comments slowly filtered into her brain.

'What happened to her girlfriend?'

'She's dead.'

'What!' Alice snapped her head towards her mother. 'When, I mean how?'

How tragic is that? The only person close to her who had died had been her father, but he was nearly seventy. To lose someone at Kerry's age must have been heartbreaking.

'Cancer.'

Alice didn't know what to say. Kerry hadn't mentioned it to her. Come to think of it, Kerry hadn't said much about her personal life full stop. Should she mention that she knew, or had Kerry told her mum in confidence?

The door opened and Kerry appeared carrying a hot drink in a white mug.

'I brought some lasagne over for my dinner, Alice, would you like some? I made too much.'

Alice turned in Kerry's direction but looked anywhere but at her face. 'Um—'

'Don't encourage her. She needs to lose a few pounds as it is,' Carol said, taking the tray from Kerry.

Kerry gave Alice a once over. 'I think she looks absolutely fine as she is.'

'What do you know? You're a nurse not a dietician.'

Alice stood. 'Let's leave her to drink her tea in peace. I'll see you tomorrow, Mum.'

Alice smiled sweetly and followed Kerry out of the room and downstairs to the kitchen.

'Thanks for sticking up for me back there,' Alice said sinking into a chair at the table.

'I was only speaking the truth, there's nothing wrong with you. You're perfect.' Kerry's face flushed and she quickly added, 'Have you been somewhere nice today?'

So she thinks I'm perfect, does she? 'Yeah, met my friend for a bit of retail therapy. Then ended up at a bar.'

'Sounds like fun,' Kerry said as she started plating up food for them both and laying the plates on the table. 'I can't remember the last time I had alcohol. I think I'd be wrecked after one drink nowadays.'

Alice laughed, failing to tell Kerry of the many bottles of wine she had shared with Stella as Kerry took a seat.

Alice picked up her fork and toyed with the food, unsure how to start the conversation about Kerry's deceased partner. In the end, she decided to be forthcoming about it.

'I don't know if you told my mum about your

partner in confidence…'

Kerry shook her head. 'No, it's fine if she told you. We were talking about death. It was an open conversation.'

'Good 'cause I don't want you to think my mum was gossiping.'

'Not at all.'

'I'm sorry for your loss,' Alice said softly.

Kerry's eyes dropped to her plate. 'I'm only glad she isn't suffering anymore.'

They ate in silence for a few minutes.

'Your mum told me a little bit about your sister,' Kerry said, putting her fork down on the side of the plate and picking up a glass of water.

Alice pushed her plate away. She'd had enough. The thought of Emily causing her to lose her appetite.

'If you'd rather not talk about it…' Kerry said apologetically.

'No, it's fine, there's just not much to say on the matter. My sister isn't the person I thought she was, simple as that. She's going to ruin my dad's reputation by airing the family's dirty laundry in a biography she's writing about him.'

Alice couldn't believe she'd told Kerry about Emily's betrayal. Not even Carol knew what Emily was in the process of doing.

Alice would be the first to admit their father was no saint, and although they had been estranged for the last few years of his life, she thought it best to let his secrets go to the grave with him and stay there.

When the biography was published and Carol got wind of it, Alice knew things were going to kick off big time. She just hoped she wasn't still around to witness it.

The pent-up tension Alice had been holding inside suddenly dissipated and she lowered her head as tears began to trickle from her eyes. She thought she was coping by pushing all of her worries deep inside, but it was obvious that wasn't the case as even more tears spilt down her cheeks.

Before Alice knew what was happening, Kerry was by her side, pulling her into a warm embrace.

'Shh, shh.' Kerry's gentle hum soothed her, causing Alice to sob even more.

Alice missed Emily and she deeply regretted not making peace with her father before he passed away. She also wanted her mother to be well enough to look after herself so she could extract herself from the toxic soup she was drowning in.

'Let me get you a tissue,' Kerry said pushing herself to her feet.

'I'm sorry.' Alice stifled a sob. She hadn't intended to cry, especially in front of Kerry, but the strain of holding the tears back had proved too much. 'I'm not normally this soppy.'

'Hey, don't be silly, we all have our moments, it's what makes us human,' Kerry said with a smile that revealed two cute dimples that Alice hadn't spotted before.

Kerry's compassion lightened her heart, for Alice

knew if she had broken down in front of her mother, Carol would have told her in no uncertain terms to pull herself together and stop being so weak-minded.

The more time Alice spent in Kerry's company, the more she realised that it was OK to be vulnerable. That to show emotion wasn't a sign of weakness after all.

It wasn't as if she hadn't worked with strong, independent women before, but there was something disruptive about Kerry. She made her feel safe and yet on edge at the same time.

Alice got to her feet, she'd said too much already and wanted to make a quick escape before she revealed how broken their family really was.

'I think I'd better call it a night. Maybe drinking wasn't such a good idea after all,' Alice said, trying to make light of the situation.

She didn't want to dump her emotional baggage on a woman who had plenty of her own worries.

'Or maybe it was just what you needed to open up,' Kerry said hesitantly. 'Look, I know it's not my place to say anything, but it's obvious you're going through a lot at the moment. Sometimes it's good to talk to someone who can be objective. What I'm trying to say is if you ever want to talk… I'm here.'

Kerry's hand briefly reached out and touched Alice's arm, causing a sudden chill to ripple along her skin.

'I appreciate that, I really do, but I'm fine. Honestly.' Ever stoic, Alice slipped into her jacket, took her phone out of her bag and ordered a cab.

'I'm just putting it out there.'

Kerry smiled and Alice couldn't help but notice her dimples again.

'Right, I'd better get a move on.'

At the front door, Alice reached for the handle and pulled the door open. Without knowing what she was going to say, she turned around to face Kerry. Alice wanted to take in every feature before she left, as if to imprint Kerry's face on her memory.

They stood opposite one another, the silence thick between them.

'I… I just want to say thanks for everything, Kerry. I was a bit doubtful about the whole idea of having someone here to help, but you've been brilliant. In more ways than one.'

Kerry blushed and pushed a stray hair behind her ear.

'You're welcome. I like working here.'

'I'm glad.' Alice smiled. 'Have a good night and if anything crops up, you've got my number, just call.'

Alice turned away again and stepped outside, walking slowly and almost reluctantly down the path.

'I will. Thanks.'

When Alice reached the gate, she turned, but Kerry had already disappeared inside and closed the door.

Wrapping her arms tightly around her waist as she waited for her cab, Alice felt a strange sense of achievement.

For the first time in her life, she was opening up

to someone and letting them see the real her. So far Kerry hadn't backed away.

Despite what her mother said, maybe, just maybe, Alice wasn't that bad after all.

Chapter Twelve

After her encounter with Alice the night before, Kerry felt even more pity for her. She seemed to be an emotional mess behind the strong façade she projected to the world. Kerry was convinced, more than ever now, that a lot of her issues had more to do with Carol than anything else, but as Debbie had warned her, if she wanted to keep her job, her only option was to view the situation from afar. Kerry knew she had no choice in the matter, especially now that her dream was finally becoming a reality. She'd had her first appointment with the fertility clinic and had gone through all the necessary checks. Once all the results were back, and she got the OK, it would be full steam ahead with her plans for the future. *A future that should have involved Sarah.*

Refusing to get caught up in the past when she had so much to look forward to in the future, Kerry tried once again to concentrate on the road ahead as she pulled out into the road. As she drove along the empty streets, her mind wandered and found its way back to Alice.

Kerry remembered her body's reaction when she'd held Alice in her arms in the hallway the night before. She knew there was something between them. A powerful surge had zapped through her veins and was unmistakeable, unmissable.

But…

There was always a but…

The chance of anything happening between them was a non-starter anyway. Carol had let on that Alice was in a long-term relationship with a woman, so how could she even think about her? Added to that, Kerry would soon be trying for a baby.

Am I going crazy? Why am I even thinking about these things?

She decided it would be best to ignore her growing attraction to Alice and concentrate solely on her job, because if she lost it, she would lose the income to finance her dream.

If ever there was a wrong time to fall for someone, this was it.

It had been a strange week – finding a new job, meeting Alice.

Then finding out Alice was already in a relationship.

And yet… the attraction was definitely reciprocated. The way Alice looked at her, those blue eyes penetrating her soul, making her crave a physical closeness that was hard to resist.

What Kerry found alluring about Alice was not just a physical attraction. She'd given it some thought during the long hours of sitting alone in the kitchen while Carol slept.

Alice was sweet, gentle and open with her emotions, something Kerry found very attractive in a woman.

She shook her head. Whatever gave her a flutter inside when she looked at Alice, Kerry would have to simply get over it.

Fifteen minutes later, Kerry stepped inside Carol's house. She was slightly disappointed Alice wasn't there. Instead, she found Mary, the next-door neighbour, sitting with Carol.

Not feeling it was her place to ask where Alice was, Kerry set about getting Carol settled down for the night. *She's probably with her girlfriend, snuggling up together, whispering sweet nothings in each other's ears.*

A hot tide of jealousy ripped through her and Kerry quickly reprimanded herself for what was an overreaction on her part. Alice had no obligation towards her. She was happy in her relationship as far as she knew.

'Did you have a good day?'

Carol let out a long sigh. 'No, I didn't. Not that my daughter cares.'

Kerry pummelled the pillows and Carol lay back against them. She had learnt to simply listen when Carol started a tirade against Alice.

'If only Emily would visit,' Carol said sadly.

Kerry's ears pricked up. That was the first time Carol had shown any kind of emotion about either daughter. Carol's expression was one of immense sadness.

'Why don't you call her?' Kerry said, suddenly feeling sorry for her.

'No point.' Carol's voice hardened. 'My own daughter, my own flesh and blood, wants nothing to do with me.'

'I find that hard to believe. Sometimes when we

have a misunderstanding, pride gets in the way.'

'You don't know Emily. She's very stubborn.'

Kerry refrained from saying, 'I wonder where she gets it from'.

It broke Kerry's heart thinking of the disconnect between Carol and her daughters. Knowing that despite her tough façade, Carol must suffer the pain of being rejected.

What if her own child did the same to her?

It gave her a source of anxiety just thinking about such a scenario.

Kerry started to update her notes in the folder on the dressing table. It was just a general observation on Carol's progress and the medication she had given her.

'Right, is there anything else I can do for you? A cup of tea perhaps?'

'No.'

'OK. Just remember, you've always got Alice.'

Just saying her name elicited an involuntary smile, and again she was reminded how much she missed Alice being there. Kerry was now accustomed to her presence upon arrival. Maybe it was a sign from the universe telling her not to get too emotionally attached.

'The one saving grace is that she'll never have to experience what I'm going through,' Carol said pitifully.

Kerry frowned, not quite understanding Carol's comment. Was she talking about having a stroke? She debated for a moment whether to enquire exactly what she meant, but before she had the chance, Carol filled her in.

'She doesn't want kids. Neither of my daughters do. I don't know why they're intent on punishing me.'

Kerry hated herself for being judgemental, but she wasn't surprised to hear this at all. Still, it saddened her that Alice would never know the joys of motherhood, no doubt because of her unstable relationship with Carol.

All Kerry knew was that when she had a child, she would make sure she did everything in her power to ensure they had a relationship with healthy boundaries in place. And she would never, never treat her child the way Carol did.

Kerry studied Carol's faraway expression and thought it best to leave the conversation where it was.

'As always, just call if you need anything.'

Kerry turned the light off and gently closed the door behind her. On her way downstairs to the kitchen, she thought about her own relationship with her parents. Though it wasn't necessarily a close one, they were civil to one another. She couldn't think of her parents doing anything to make her turn her back on them, which made her wonder what exactly Carol had done for Emily to hold such bitterness and resentment against her own parents.

Chapter Thirteen

Fatigue oozed from every pore as Alice's heavy eyelids slowly drooped and she gently dozed off into an unconscious void. She only realised she had succumbed to sleep when her eyes were forced open again by the incessant ringing of her phone. Becoming instantly alert in case it was an emergency, Alice reached down to grab her jacket. After a quick root through her pockets, she located the phone and pressed the screen to accept the call, only registering that it was Izzy when it was too late to decline.

'What do you want?' Alice said, realising how harsh that sounded as the words escaped, unbidden, from her lips.

'Hi, yourself,' Izzy said, unperturbed by the hostility in Alice's voice. 'I just heard about your mum. How is she? How're you?'

Alice was impressed Izzy sounded so sincere. She couldn't help but wonder how Izzy had found out, given that she hadn't told anyone.

'She's OK. We both are.' Alice realised that she'd hardly thought about Izzy since meeting Kerry.

'Are you sure?'

'Positive. It was a mild stroke. She'll be fine,' Alice said, not really wanting to get involved in a long, drawn out conversation.

'I'm glad to hear it. Look, I'd really like to see her.'

Alice groaned inwardly. Her mum adored Izzy. She'd be annoyed if Alice thwarted her chance to catch up. *And no doubt slag me off.*

Although Alice desperately wanted to say a long loud 'No' down the phone and hang up on her, she reluctantly said, 'OK, I think Mum would appreciate that, but I don't see that there's anything for us to talk about.'

'I… I thought you should know… I've broken up with Judith…'

Alice's eyes widened. 'So much for her being the love of your life.'

'I could really do with a friend right now.'

Alice snorted. 'I've told you how I feel about that. If you want to see my mum that's fine but anything else, forget it.'

Silence.

'When do you want to come 'round?' Alice said, anxious to end the call.

'Some time this week, I'll drop by when I can.'

'OK. Look, I haven't told my mum we split up for obvious reasons, so I'd appreciate you not mentioning it to her.' There was a sharp tone in her voice again, but she couldn't help it.

'I understand you not wanting to worry her. Besides, we might get—'

Alice knew what Izzy was going to say. *Never in a million years would I get back with you!*

'I've got to go. I'll see you soon.'

'Oh OK.'

Alice cut the call without saying goodbye.

She dropped the phone onto the empty space beside her and slowly let out the breath she didn't realise she'd been holding. To her surprise, it only took a few minutes to get over the shock of Izzy's admission that she had turned Alice's life upside down for a relationship that hadn't even lasted five minutes.

All thoughts of Izzy soon forgotten, Alice turned on her side and promptly fell asleep.

***

The morning couldn't have come soon enough. Alice even arrived at her mother's house an hour earlier than usual. She hadn't seen Kerry since the previous week as she'd decided to put some much-needed distance between herself and Carol. Alice had asked Carol's next-door neighbour to go in and sit with Carol until Kerry arrived for her night shift.

For the first time ever, Alice did not feel the slightest bit of guilt for avoiding her mother. Their last encounter had made sure of that. Besides, having more time during the day gave her the opportunity to plan her itinerary for her upcoming trip.

Her initial plan was to go for a year, but she had now decided to travel indefinitely. Maybe return to the UK once a year to visit her mum and take flowers to her father's grave.

Pushing open the front door, Alice strolled into the kitchen with two large mixed bunches of flowers, and a bag full of snacks and cakes which she picked up almost without thinking in the supermarket while she wandered around in a daze.

'Let me help you with some of those,' Kerry said as she entered.

'Thanks, where's Mum?' Alice asked quietly as she handed the flowers over to Kerry.

'Asleep on the sofa in the living room. She hasn't been sleeping well these past few nights,' Kerry said.

Since I stopped visiting. No surprise there. 'I hope she hasn't been a pain in the arse.'

'No, she's been incredibly quiet,' Kerry said, a look of concern in her eyes.

How could Alice explain to Kerry that this was yet just another one of her mother's mind games. Something she did to draw attention to herself when she didn't get her own way. Or if, God forbid, Alice's life didn't revolve around her.

In the end, she decided not to bother. No one understood what she went through with her mother and she was tired of trying to explain.

'I wouldn't worry about it. From as far back as I remember, she's always been a bad sleeper,' Alice said.

'Oh, I thought it was because she was worried about something.'

'If that were the case, she'd never sleep. My mum's a natural born worrier.' Alice held up the shopping bag. 'Have you got time for breakfast? I'm starving and I brought treats. Danish pastries, doughnuts, and heaven knows what else.'

'Sure, I have an appointment at ten, so I've got time to kill.' Kerry's bright smile lit up her face. 'Anything I can do to help?'

'Tell you what. In that cupboard over there, there are a couple of vases. You arrange the flowers and I'll sort breakfast.'

Alice busied herself in the kitchen, passing through a pitcher of water for the flowers, and dutifully putting together croissants on one plate and a selection of the treats on another, then bringing them through just as Kerry finished placing the last vase on a windowsill.

'Oh, they look great. Much better in here now. Really brightens the place up. You've done an excellent job. Maybe you should consider a new career as a florist?'

Kerry snapped her head around. 'You don't mean—'

'Ha-ha, no I don't mean you're doing a bad job here, far from it, just that you have a good eye for flower arranging. Come on, sit.'

Kerry joined Alice at the table, and they swapped stories of their mornings.

While Kerry busied herself with the food on her plate, Alice's gaze was once again drawn to her mouth, imagining what it would feel like to kiss her sensual lips, gently nipping her bottom lip between her teeth then slowly sliding her tongue inside her mouth…

'Are you OK? You look like you're a million miles away,' Kerry said.

Alice gave a quick shake of her head upon hearing Kerry's voice and rapidly came back to the present moment.

'What? Oh, sorry. I was just thinking about something.'

She gave her an enquiring look and Alice sighed. She couldn't tell Kerry she was fantasising about her, but she could let her know about the call she'd received the night before.

'My ex. She called me last night.'

'Ex?' Kerry said. 'Your mum said you had a girlfriend?'

'Yeah. I did. We recently broke up.' Alice took a sip of tea. 'She found out about Mum having a stroke and wants to see her.'

So Kerry knows I'm gay too.

Carol had clearly made sure Kerry knew Alice was attached. That explained the comment about only having one true love. She was indirectly telling Alice to keep away from Kerry.

'Don't you want her to come?'

'It would be nice for my mum to see her again, but I'm not sure I want to.'

'Is that because you're still in love with her?'

When she spoke, Alice realised Kerry averted her gaze.

'No, I just don't like loose ends. Our relationship is over. I don't want her walking in and out of my life when she feels like it.'

'So why didn't you just say no?' Kerry asked.

Alice stared at her perplexed. The truth was, she really didn't know. She shrugged unable to answer. Was it because she agreed to most things due to not liking confrontation? Probably.

'It was easier to say yes, I suppose.'

Kerry looked thoughtful for a moment.

'Maybe you should talk to your mum, make sure she understands what's happened and ask her if she wants to see...' Kerry drew out the word.

'Izzy,' Alice said.

'...Izzy. Given that you've broken up, she might not want to see her.'

'Knowing my mum, she'll probably blame me for the breakup even though it was down to Izzy.' Alice allowed a wry smile to cross her face. 'Anyway, that's why I looked distracted.'

'And that's all?'

The moment was loaded and for a second Alice thought about telling Kerry the truth, but in the end, she lost her nerve and simply said, 'Yes, that's all.'

Chapter Fourteen

Kerry was petrified.

The closer she got to 'Pregnancy Start Fertility' the worse her stomach churned.

The Sat Nav informed her she would be at her destination in fifteen minutes.

Fifteen minutes.

Her appointment would take an hour, after which she would walk out of the building and her life as she knew it could be well and truly over. Was she ready for this?

Ten minutes.

Beads of perspiration prickled her forehead then her temples as the salty droplets slowly trickled down the side of her face.

What am I so worried about? She'd been asking herself the same question since she'd left Carol's house earlier. *This is what I want, isn't it?*

Kerry had gone over the calculations a trillion times both in her head and on paper – both showed the same result. With the money she was earning at Carol's, and the savings she had put aside, she could most definitely afford to have a child.

Seven minutes.

The speed limit was 30mph. Kerry drove at 20mph.

Was she deliberately trying to make herself late? Sabotage herself so she would have to rebook it? And then what? What if she still had doubts a week from today? A month? A year? By going ahead, Kerry was committing herself to a minimum of eighteen years, but in reality, a lifetime of caring for the person she gave birth to.

Could she commit to that? Deeply commit? It was such a huge undertaking, and she would be doing it entirely alone.

Three minutes.

A finger of fear crept through her, wrapping itself around her spine, making her inwardly shudder. What if she was a terrible mother? What if the child was horrible?

What if, what if, what if. The problems kept mounting.

What if she didn't go through with it and regretted it for the rest of her life?

Kerry let her attention rest on that question for a few moments and knew what she was doing was the right thing.

You have arrived at your destination.

Kerry eased her car into the small carpark and turned off the engine. Glancing at the digital clock, she was relieved to see she was ten minutes early. That gave her enough time to prepare herself. Turn off the negative voices in her head that were doing their upmost to drown out the positive ones.

Yes, the child could turn out to be the devil's spawn, but it could also be the most amazing little being in the world.

The numbers on the clock had moved several ticks

during the time she'd been having an internal discussion with herself.

It was decision time. To back out or go full steam ahead.

Kerry found herself reaching for the door handle and opened the door. Climbing out of the car, she turned and locked it, almost mechanically and trance-like.

She stared at the small nondescript building up ahead, whose consultants had the power to change someone's life. *My life.*

Within minutes, Kerry entered the reception room where blackout blinds concealed the windows from the dark clouds on the horizon outside. The walls painted varying shades of yellow gave the illusion of being a bigger space than it was. Kerry glanced around the room at posters of smiling mothers and new-born babies that were displayed on the walls, giving the impression anything was possible when it came to helping women with fertility issues.

It was just the kind of reassurance she needed to see.

Ten minutes later, Kerry sat opposite her consultant, Michael Evans. A handsome man in his late fifties. His white smile and tanned leather skin looked out of place – he belonged in sunny L.A. not an unglamorous, cloudy town like Guildford.

His voice was deep and husky as he went through what she was to expect, and the company's policies. Kerry nodded in response, not completely taking it all in. She just wanted the procedure over now. She knew what she was committing herself to and nothing Mr Evans said would make her change her mind.

'Are you ready?' His voice seemed to come from a million miles away.

Kerry dutifully nodded. It was odd being on the other side of the fence, where she was now the patient, her future in the hands of a stranger.

The door opened behind her and she heard a female voice asking her to follow.

Did she smile at Dr Evans in thanks? Kerry couldn't remember as she hurriedly left the room and followed Mel, as her name tag spelt, down the pastel-coloured hallway to a doorway at the end.

Kerry hesitated to peer into the narrow room with its metallic bed and thick mattress covered by a dazzling white sheet and plumped up pillow. The silver clinical stirrups beside the bed caused Kerry's breath to suspend momentarily as her heart raced.

Mel smiled at her from inside the room. Encouragement in the tenderness of her gaze. She'd probably been through this a million times with other women.

Desperate women. Unsure women. Nervous women. *Scared women.*

Kerry took a step forward. Followed by another, then another, gradually pushing away the blind panic gnawing at her.

Soon she was out of her work clothes and wearing a green gown, climbing unsteadily onto the bed. Dr Evans entered, looking ever the professional as he checked his chart and spoke a few words to Mel in hushed tones.

Kerry lay back on the bed and closed her eyes, bringing up a vision of Sarah in her mind's eye to comfort her. She blocked out the activity going on around her and imagined their happier times together when Sarah had been fit and healthy. Her laughter. Her love.

'All done,' Dr Evans informed her once the procedure was over.

Sarah's fertilised egg was inside of her.

Kerry would be bringing a part of Sarah to life.

Chapter Fifteen

'Where're you going?' Alice said, grinning at Stella who was gripping a tall glass of gin and tonic.

A holiday would do her the world of good, Alice decided. After their last chat, Alice had been more sensitive to Stella's mood and couldn't believe she had missed the signs that something was wrong. Normally, they were so in tune with one another's emotions.

'A retreat—'

'Nice,' Alice said, imagining all the back massages, pampering and yoga.

'I'll be gone for ten days.'

Alice jumped in. 'Jesus, Stella, that's a bit long isn't it? I mean, I know you're feeling down, but could you really put up with someone fussing over you for ten days?'

'It's not that kind of retreat, Alice.'

Alice looked at her perplexed. 'Eh?'

'It's a meditation retreat. Silence for ten days.'

'What! You're not joking, are you?'

Stella traced her fingertip around the rim of her glass. 'No. I've spoken to Fred.'

'And?' Alice asked, wondering what on earth Stella could have told him to soften the blow of her dropping out of their marriage for ten days having never spent a night apart. Knowing Fred the way she did, and his insecurities, abandonment was something he wouldn't take lightly. Even if it was under the guise of saving their marriage.

'I told him I need time to find myself, and he agreed if that was what I needed, so be it.'

'Really? Wow. I mean I'm surprised he took it so well.'

'He didn't have much of a say in the matter. This is about my life and what I need. I'm not going to end up on the scrap heap, whether addicted to prescription pills or booze.'

'That's great then, but I'm gonna miss you like mad,' Alice said.

Her biggest fear was that by the time Stella returned from her retreat, she would be long gone. Living her new life. She couldn't wait.

'I'll miss you too, but hopefully I'll come back a better person.'

'That would be impossible. You're perfect just the way you are.'

'You're such a sweetie,' Stella said. 'Anyway, back to you. Do you really think letting Izzy, that cheating bitch, back in your life is wise?'

'What choice do I have?' Alice threw her hands in the air. 'I can't stop her from seeing my mum.'

Stella eyed Alice as if she had lost her mind. 'Who said you can't?'

Alice let out an exaggerated sigh. 'If I'm honest, Izzy isn't the issue.'

'Oh,' Stella said, raising her eyebrows.

Alice was bored of talking about Izzy. Time to

move on to her favourite subject.

'If I weren't tipsy, I wouldn't be telling you this now.'

Stella leant forward with raised eyebrows. 'Go on, I'm all ears.'

'It's my mum's nurse…'

Stella gasped, covering her hand with her mouth. 'You think the nurse is abusing you're mu—'

'What! No, of course not!'

'So why'd you look so distressed?' Stella's expression of shock slowly changed into one of glee. 'You've got the hots for her, haven't you?'

'That and I can't get her out of my mind. It's like I've got an obsession about her.'

It was becoming a serious worry that most of Alice's thoughts over the past forty-eight hours were of Kerry and little else.

'Limerence,' Stella stated matter-of-factly, before taking a mouthful of wine.

'What the hell is that?'

'Invasive thinking about someone.'

Alice pulled a face. 'Isn't that just a fancy name for a crush or infatuation?'

Stella inhaled and exhaled in quick succession. 'Nope, this fucker can make you suicidal once it has its grip on you.'

'I don't feel suicidal, Stella.'

'Not yet you don't. Honestly, some of my clients have felt they were on the verge of madness.'

'Trust me, it isn't that bad. I just like her. A lot.'

Alice looked down at her empty glass and wondered whether or not to refill it. The thought of a lingering hangover the next day wasn't enough to stop her in the end.

'The most important question first… is she gay?'

'Yes, and that's the problem.' Alice refilled half a glass. 'Her partner died. I don't think she wants to date again.'

'Is that what she said?'

'Well, no.'

'So how d'you know what she wants?' Stella sounded amused.

'It just stands to reason, doesn't it? I mean if my partner died, I don't think I'd ever be able to look at another woman again.'

'Now you're projecting. She's not you. Just because you feel that way doesn't mean she does.'

'But it's not just that. I want to go travelling once my mum's back on her feet.' Alice sighed at the thought of no longer requiring Kerry's services.

'Seems like someone's just looking for any excuse to not get involved.'

'That's not true.'

Heat slowly made its way up to Alice's cheeks and settled there. Stella smiled at her reaction. Blushing had been Alice's trademark ever since she could remember. She'd always been a hopeless liar, and the fact she looked a bit like a Belisha beacon when she embellished the truth was a dead giveaway.

'D'you want to sleep with her?' Stella asked.

'No!' was Alice's suitably shocked reply. Almost immediately wishing she hadn't said a word about her. 'That's the problem, I don't know what I want from her.'

***

An hour later, and not wanting to wake Emily, Alice decided to crash at her mum's house. Kerry would still be awake, so it wasn't as if she'd disturb her. Well, that's what Alice told herself. The truth was that she wanted to see Kerry again.

By the time she arrived at her mother's, Alice regretted her overreaction and, having thought about it, realised that she might be guilty of wanting to sleep with Kerry, but at the same time worrying that in effect, it would be a bit Downtonian. Maybe that was why she had reacted so badly back at the bar. That and the four glasses of wine!

As Alice walked up the path after being dropped off by a taxi, she was slightly surprised to see multiple lights glaring away in the house. It was 1 a.m. She hurried a little quicker along the drive. Lights should not be glaring at one in the morning.

The house should be locked up tight and the lights should be off.

Alice started to feel just a little queasy. Had something happened?

Fumbling with her keys made things worse, and by the time she slotted her key in the lock and opened the door, enough noise had been made to wake the dead.

Alice shut the door behind her just slightly too quickly, leaving it rattling in the door frame.

The sudden appearance of Kerry made her jump.

Kerry held a finger over her lips and waved Alice forward, eventually closing the door behind her and ushering her into the kitchen.

'Why are all the lights still on?' Alice asked just the tiniest bit too intensely.

Kerry couldn't hide the smile on her face. 'Your mum freaked out when she saw a mouse.'

Alice pulled a face. 'Yuck?'

'Did you find it?'

'It took me a while, but I managed to get it into a box and release it.'

Alice reached out, briefly laying her hand on Kerry's shoulder. 'Ah you're so sweet and caring.'

Kerry's cheeks turned crimson. 'What're you doing here?'

'I've been out with my friend. I can't find my keys and I didn't want to wake my sister. She's one of those people that gets majorly pissed off if their sleep is disturbed,' Alice said, gingerly holding on to the wall for support. 'So, I thought I'd kip in the spare room.'

'D'you think you should have some coffee?'

'I'd sooner have a brandy,' Alice said, swaying slightly.

Kerry laughed. 'I'll make you some coffee. By the looks of things, you've probably had enough to drink tonight.'

'I only had four glasses of wine… I think it was four.' The reality was that she'd actually lost count after their second bottle. 'Oh, all right, Miss Bossy.'

Kerry briefly glanced around as she headed down the hallway.

By the time the coffee arrived, Alice could barely keep her eyes open, although she did try and perk up when Kerry deposited a cup of hot strong coffee in front of her. But it was pointless. The room swam before her eyes and, not that she was complaining, there were two of Kerry instead of one.

'Thanks, Kerry.' Alice tried to pick the mug up, but it tilted towards her, threatening to spill over.

'Come on, I think I'd better put you to bed.'

Alice's spirits sunk at the thought of the night ending before it had begun. 'Whatever you say.'

'Let's just try and get you upstairs without making too much noise, eh?'

Alice stifled a giggle at the thought of going to bed with her mum's nurse.

'What's funny?' Kerry asked, gently lowering Alice onto the bed.

Alice's gaze travelled over Kerry's face and searched her eyes. An intensity flared through her entrancement as the realisation hit her of how incredibly beautiful Kerry was, and it wasn't the beer goggles talking either. Alice had thought so from the very first time they met.

Heat edged its way up her neck. 'Oh nothing, I was just thinking of something my friend said.'

'Wanna share?'

Alice shook her head and pulled the cover up to her chin. She might be drunk, but she wasn't so drunk she'd tell Kerry she'd lied to Stella.

Her gaze dropped from Kerry's eyes, to the nape of her neck, to her breasts.

I do want to sleep with her.

The thought of lying naked with Kerry made Alice's heart jolt against her chest and her pulse pound in rapid succession.

Closing her eyes, Alice exhaled a pent-up breath in a long sigh. The reality of the situation left her desolate with an inexplicable sense of emptiness residing in every part of her body.

Mainly her heart.

Chapter Sixteen

Emily checked the clock for what would have been the tenth time that night. It was twenty past two in the morning and there was no sign of Alice. Not that she was keeping tabs on her, but Alice would normally have been back by now. Since Alice had arrived, she hadn't stayed out any later than midnight, and that was only because she was doing a change over with the nurse she'd hired. The drive over from their mum's house wouldn't take more than half an hour. Begrudgingly, Emily checked the local traffic report to see if there had been any accidents, and to her relief, there hadn't.

As much as she would like to call Alice to check her whereabouts, the stubbornness of Emily's nature forbade it. To do so would imply she cared, which at that moment in time, she preferred to pretend not to.

What did caring get you? A whole load of heartache.

Emily was so done with being hurt by thoughtless, uncaring people. So she would stay in her bubble of anger because it served to keep her guard up and, most importantly, people away from her. It was almost as if they could sense she would hypothetically bite without barking first.

She'd tried so hard to not think about the conversation she'd had with Arnold. She had no time for enablers. And that's what he was by siding with her father. The worst thing was that all these years she'd stupidly thought Arnold agreed with her.

Putting loyalty aside, what if Arnold went to her publisher and told them his version of the truth? Who would they believe? The best friend of a man the nation adored, or the daughter whose poisoned words made him out to be the devil incarnate?

Maybe I shouldn't have been so dismissive of Arnold.

Maybe she should have listened to what he had to say, or at least pretended to. Instead, Emily was now ashamed to admit, she had been dismissive to the point of rudeness and he had made a hasty exit as quickly as his frail legs would carry him.

In the heat of the moment, Emily took out her phone and found Arnold's number in her contact list. At least she'd had the common sense to ask for his details in case she needed to get in touch with him. Despite the lateness of the hour, Emily typed a text message into her phone.

If you still want to talk forward me your address and I'll come and see you.

Without giving herself the chance to backtrack, Emily firmly pressed the send button. She couldn't expect Arnold to make another journey from Hertfordshire. He'd already told her it had taken him two hours to get to her house.

No, it was best she went to him. Only this time she would actually listen to what he had to say. Well, at least pretend to. She would nod and say all the right things in the right places to appease him, but once she left, she would forget every rotten lie that came out of his mouth.

And she would forget Arnold as well.

After they spoke again, he would be as dead to her as her own father.

Chapter Seventeen

Alice was still asleep when Kerry let herself out of the house early the next morning. Carol's neighbour had come to sit with her, so she was free to go. Kerry couldn't quite make out what caused the butterflies in the pit of her stomach. Was it Alice's sudden appearance the night before and the opportunity it had presented to be in close proximity to her? Or was it that in a matter of weeks, she would find out if she was pregnant?

Kerry tried her hardest not to think too much about what was in store for the future, if the actual procedure itself worked. If it did, there'd be nine months of feeling a part of Sarah growing inside of her, and then finally she would meet him or her.

Too buoyed up with excitement to go home and sleep, Kerry made a quick call to Debbie and was soon on her way to the hospital canteen.

'You look knackered,' was the first thing Debbie said upon seeing her as she made her way over to her table. 'But you have a certain glow about you. Are you happy?'

'Very.' Kerry unconsciously smoothed her hair out of her face as she sat down with her cup of coffee. 'More than I've been in a long time.'

Debbie leant across the table and squeezed her hand. 'I'm glad. If anyone deserves to be happy it's you.'

'There are much more deserving people out—'

'Just stop. I'm not talkin' about other people. I'm talkin' about you. For once, please understand that it's OK for you to have a piece of happy pie without deprivin' anyone else of anythin',' Debbie said.

'Yes, Mum.'

'Good! Now that's settled, tell me how things are goin'. It feels like I haven't seen you for an age.'

'You OK?' Kerry asked, suddenly taking in Debbie's sullen demeanour. 'Has something happened?'

'Yeah, but it's not somethin' I can't handle.'

'I hope it's nothing serious.'

Debbie rolled her eyes. 'Nah, unless you consider livin' next door to a couple of swingers, shaggin' in the garden serious.'

Kerry bit her lip to stifle a smile. 'Please tell me you're kidding?'

'I wish I was. By the time I got to the window after hearin' Kev call me, they had their dildos out and were doin' God knows what with them.'

'Jesus Christ!' Kerry couldn't restrain herself any longer and a burst of laughter escaped her mouth. She quickly covered it with her hand. 'I'm sorry, I shouldn't laugh, have people no shame?'

'Obviously not. Kev wanted to go 'round and give 'em a piece of his mind, but I had to stop him. You know he's got a temper. The last thing I need is him gettin' locked up.'

'I can't say I would've blamed him,' Kerry said, trying her hardest not to laugh again. 'You should've called the police.'

'They wouldn't care. They're doin' it in their own home. Kev said he's gonna record them next time and upload it to YouTube.' Debbie laughed at the thought. 'Anyway, enough about me, what's happenin' with the baby situation?'

'I did it.' Kerry blurted out before she could stop herself. She'd wanted to keep it secret until the results confirmed it, but she was too happy. She needed to share her news with someone and who better than her best friend.

Debbie crossed her arms tightly over her chest. 'What! Why didn't you tell me?'

'In case it doesn't work.'

Debbie's expression softened. 'Don't be silly, of course it'll work… So we may have a mini-Kerry in the world in nine months. I can't wait!'

Now was the best time to reveal all. Kerry hadn't told Debbie of her plans before because she didn't know how she'd take it.

'The baby won't exactly be a mini me.'

Debbie looked at her questioningly. 'Meaning?'

'Meaning that I'm using one of Sarah's eggs.'

For a moment, Debbie merely gawped at her. The slackening of her jaw and widened eyes a great giveaway at her disbelief, and then very slowly Debbie's eyes welled with tears. When one spilt over and ran down her cheek, Debbie roughly wiped it away with the back of her hand.

'I don't know what to say.'

'That you're happy for me,' Kerry said tentatively,

keeping her eyes fixed on the coffee cup in front of her. Kerry didn't know what she'd expected Debbie to say, but her response surprised her. Were her tears ones of joy? Or did she pity Kerry for still desperately trying to hold on to a piece of Sarah after all this time.

'Please say something. Even if it's to call me an idiot, or to tell me I've lost my mind.'

Much to her relief, Debbie was soon on her feet and pulling Kerry up to join her. 'Happy for you? I'm ecstatic. I can't believe it! Why didn't you tell me?'

Kerry's voice was muffled. 'Because I didn't know if I was going to go through with it.'

'Everythin' and I mean everythin', pales into insignificance compared to this.'

Kerry blinked back the tears welling in her eyes.

In the midst of her joy, her mind still managed to circle back to Alice, the woman she barely knew but whose opinion she cared very much about. What would she think of the situation?

Nothing, Kerry realised with a start. Alice probably never gave her a second thought as soon as she was out of sight. It was Kerry who was the one that couldn't stop thinking of Alice whenever her mind was unguarded. Why did she find it so hard to keep her emotions in check? More importantly, why was this happening to her now when she had so many other things that needed her full attention?

'I want you to know, no sorry, I want *both* of you to know that Aunty Debbie is going to be there for you through thick and thin.'

'Thanks, Debs.' That was exactly what she needed to hear, there would be no support from anywhere else. Her so called friends had fallen to the wayside when Sarah had become ill, and after she died, either through embarrassment of not being there when she needed them, or simply lack of care, they didn't return.

'So how long you got left at your current job?'

Heat cautiously crept up to her cheeks and Kerry hoped she'd put on enough blusher to hide the tell-tale sign. She picked up her coffee mug and made a show of blowing on it even though it was no longer hot, but she needed to buy some time.

Should she go the full mile and tell her about her unexpected feelings towards Alice or would two confessions in the space of ten minutes prove too much for her friend?

Seconds ticked by until Kerry finally decided it was best not to say anything about Alice.

Not yet anyway.

Chapter Eighteen

Alice opened the front door and immediately held her finger in mid-air, signalling to Izzy that she had to take a call. Although Alice had been expecting her, she was surprised by her own response to Izzy's appearance on her mother's doorstep. She felt nothing. As if Izzy was merely an acquaintance popping around for a drink.

'Hi, yes, I'm good thanks,' Alice said into the phone as she waved Izzy in. Ellen sounded fretful as she explained her predicament. She had a family emergency to attend to so wouldn't be able to visit. 'Of course, it'll be fine. No, don't worry I'll let Mum know. OK, see you in a few days. Take care. Bye.'

When Alice disconnected the call, she went in search of Izzy who was now in the kitchen making herself a coffee as if it was her home.

'Who was that?' Izzy asked nonchalantly, as she poured boiling water into a mug.

'Ellen,' Alice said despite herself. Who she spoke to was no longer any of Izzy's business and she'd do well to remember that.

'Oh right. So how's your mum doing?'

'Much better. She was up and about earlier today.'

'That's good.' Izzy looked genuinely pleased with the news. 'It must've been scary for you. Does she still have a carer looking after her?'

'She has a nurse. She works the night shift.' When

Izzy raised her eyebrows, Alice added begrudgingly, 'I'm still a bit apprehensive about leaving her alone.'

'She can't have a babysitter forever.'

'Don't you think I know that?' Alice snapped. She didn't know what had caused her sudden irritation, Izzy interfering or the realisation that she would have to part ways with Kerry soon. If Alice had her own way, this cosy little set up would never end.

'Can I see her?' Izzy said, looking at her expectantly.

'Who?' Alice's voice was almost shrill at the thought of Izzy meeting Kerry. She didn't want the waters muddied by her presence. It was only when she saw Izzy look at her questioningly that she realised Izzy was referring to her mother. 'Oh, my mum. Yeah right. Of course.'

'Who else did you think I was talking about?'

'Uh no one.' It gave Alice momentary satisfaction to see curiosity cross Izzy's features.

At one point in their lives, Alice would have kept nothing from Izzy. Not even her birthday surprises which always angered Izzy to the point where she'd rage that there was no point in even celebrating her birthday as there simply wouldn't be anything to surprise her with. Thinking back now, Alice couldn't believe how much she'd tolerated in their relationship. Izzy behaved like an overprivileged child.

And to think I thought I was happy with her? I must have been desperate! Or mad.

'Alice…' Izzy lowered her eyes. I—'

'Come on, my mum's upstairs,' Alice said briskly,

interrupting her before she could say another word. Alice knew what was coming and she wanted to avoid it at all costs. She had no time for Izzy's platitudes.

Already anxiously awaiting Kerry's arrival, Alice hurried out of the kitchen and to her mother's room. It was better to get Izzy's visit over with before they went around in circles – they'd already done enough of that.

Izzy followed close behind in silence. Alice could almost feel her gaze boring into her arse as she mounted the stairs. It was, or should she say used to be, Izzy's favourite part of her body.

Carol pulled her covers back in an attempt to climb out of her bed at the sight of Izzy.

'No, don't get up,' Izzy said, rushing to her side and embracing her.

'Well aren't you a sight for sore eyes. Why didn't you tell me Izzy was visiting?' Carol said, leaning back from the embrace to stare at Alice.

'I wanted it to be a surprise.'

'Full of secrets that one is,' Carol said, patting the empty space beside her. 'How've you been?'

'Not too bad. I'm glad to see you looking well,' Izzy said, slipping out of her jacket.

Alice sighed. This was not a good sign. Izzy looked like she was going to be there for the night. Alice checked her watch again for what must have been the tenth time since Izzy arrived.

Shit! Kerry would be there in half an hour. What should she do? She couldn't ask Izzy to leave as her mum would wonder why. Alice still hadn't found the courage to tell her mum they'd broken up. At first it had been because she hadn't wanted to worry her or add any more stress to the situation, but over time it was simply because Izzy no longer occupied any part of her mind.

The emptiness and sense of loneliness she thought would overwhelm her just never materialised. Well, it was too late to tell her now. Alice would wait a few days and let it slip that things hadn't worked out between them for a number of reasons.

She wouldn't tell her the real one. Not even Alice could shatter the illusion her mother had of Izzy, who she thought of as a second daughter.

The two chatted as if Alice was invisible which she didn't mind as it meant she could slip away unnoticed when the front door gently closed downstairs. Kerry was early.

A ghost of a smile curved Alice's lips and she had to refrain from running down the stairs to greet her. Forcing herself to take one step at a time, Kerry was still in the hallway hanging up her jacket when Alice finally reached the bottom of the stairs.

Kerry turned around, her eyes gazing intently into her own, drawing her in. There was something different about them today. They seemed to glow.

In that moment, no words were spoken or needed. Not even a hello. The atmosphere surrounding them taut with an electrical current.

Alice briefly dropped her eyes to Kerry's mouth, wanting desperately to kiss her more than ever now.

The desire for her which had been growing steadily

had now reached its peak.

'I wasn't expecting you to be here,' Kerry said as she took a step towards Alice.

The sound of Izzy's voice floating down from the top of the stairs broke the spell. Kerry looked up the staircase questioningly.

'Izzy,' Alice said.

'Oh.' Kerry stepped back and rummaged through her bag as footsteps sounded down the stairs. She finally withdrew a thick folder.

'Ellen couldn't make it today.'

'Oh, right.'

Kerry was close enough now that Alice had to fight the urge to reach out and touch her. Even if it was her shoulder or her forearm. She just wanted, no needed, physical contact with her. But there wasn't any reason that called for it, nor was there time.

'Hello.' Izzy walked up behind Alice.

Though Kerry smiled, there was a look of unease in her eyes. 'Hi.'

'I'm Izzy.'

'Kerry.'

The women shook hands and Alice felt a stab of jealousy that Izzy got to touch her while she couldn't.

'The nurse. Carol was just telling me all about you.'

'All good I hope.'

'Of course, but what they both forgot to tell me was how gorgeous you are.'

Alice inwardly squirmed at Izzy's blatant flirting. It was yet another attribute she had forgotten. Izzy always had an eye for a pretty woman. Not that Alice didn't, but at least she looked for similar values and substance. Kerry had both in bucket loads.

To Alice's delight, Kerry acknowledged Izzy's comment with nothing more than a tight-lipped smile.

'I'd better go and see how my patient is getting on,' Kerry said side-stepping the women and making her way up the stairs.

'So that's why you've been so quiet eh?' Izzy narrowed her eyes. It wasn't a question, it was an accusation. 'The sexy nurse has captured your attention.'

'Shhh.' Alice grabbed Izzy by the arm and frogmarched her to the kitchen, praying Kerry hadn't heard Izzy's comment. 'She'll hear you.'

'So?'

Kerry closed the door behind them. 'So? She's my mum's nurse. The last thing she needs to be thinking is that I fancy her.'

'But you do, right?'

'What are you on about?' Alice crossed the room and made a start on loading the

dishwasher. Once that was finished, she'd get out the mop and clean the floor, even though it didn't need doing. At this stage, Alice would do anything to avoid having to sit down and converse with Izzy about her feelings for Kerry. Hell, she'd only just about admitted having them to herself, so she was hardly going to start blabbing her mouth off to Izzy of all people.

'Come on, Alice. I know you, remember? If I recall, the way you look at her is how you once looked at me.'

'Once being the operative word,' Alice said under her breath.

'Not that I blame you. She really is quite scrumptious.'

Alice slammed the dishwasher door shut and looked up at her. 'Scrumptious? She's a grown woman, Izzy, not a slice of lemon drizzle cake.'

'OK, so she's hot.'

'And my mum's nurse,' Alice reminded her again.

'Not for long though.'

Alice froze.

'Your mum said another week and she's off to visit her sister in France. Tickets have already been booked.'

'What?' A week! *One more week of seeing Kerry and then what?*

Izzy frowned. 'She didn't tell you?'

'No, she didn't,' Alice muttered.

Her hand unconsciously formed into a tight fist when, from the room directly above, she could hear muted chatter and laughter followed by the sound of Kerry moving around on the wooden floorboards.

What the hell was her mum playing at? By the sounds of it, she must have been planning this for a while. And what of Kerry? Did she know about her mother's decision? If she did, she didn't seem that bothered about moving on, which to Alice's mind meant that the mutual attraction she thought they'd both shared was in her head.

I'm a fool. A stupid fool!

'Hey, don't look so despondent,' Izzy said as if

reading her mind. 'I'll see if I can get her number. Once I'm done with her, you can have her.'

'Do you have to be so vile?'

'It was a joke, Alice. You know… a ha ha moment.'

'Well it's not funny.' Alice had quite enough for one day. 'Look, I think it's time you left. Kerry will want to lock up for the night soon.'

'OK, anyway, I told your mum I'd visit again in a couple of days. I take it you'll be here?'

'Yes, I'll be here.' Alice would be damned if she was going to give Izzy the opportunity to spend any alone time with Kerry.

'See you soon then.'

Without another word, Izzy left and moments later the front door slammed. A month ago, it would have been unthinkable to be glad to see Izzy leave, but now, if Alice never saw her again as long as she lived, she would be OK with that.

Why was fate so cruel to her? Why, if Alice couldn't have Kerry, had she come into her life in the first place?

Chapter Nineteen

Up until now, the faceless person Alice had been in love with was the very attractive woman Kerry had unexpectedly come face to face with in the hallway. Although Alice had pre-warned Kerry of Izzy's impending visit, she still hadn't been prepared for the raw emotion it stirred up in her. It had been a double whammy in the space of five minutes.

First, she'd had the surprise of Alice being there when she'd arrived. Her tight-fitted vest accentuating her moderately-sized breasts really hadn't help stem the rush of hormones making a mad dash through her body, or the fact that Alice's delicate arms led down to elegant hands that Kerry couldn't help but wish were wandering all over her—especially her—*Oh God, My hormones are getting out of control!*

They may well have been, but God it was so good to see Alice again. Kerry hadn't realised how much she missed her after not seeing her for four days.

She pined for her. That was probably why Kerry was feeling the way she was. She knew there was power in naming the emotion she was experiencing. Name it and sit with it until the feeling passed which it normally did within a few minutes. It was a mindful technique Kerry had been taught from her grief counsellor after Sarah died.

While Kerry double checked Carol was comfortable in bed, she internalised her thoughts and the emotions swimming through her.

Jealousy.

Though Kerry knew she had no claim on Alice whatsoever, she couldn't stop the green-eyed monster raising its head at the thought of Alice and Izzy together. They were well suited. Alice being a brunette. Izzy a blonde. Even their bodies were similar. A match made in heaven. Which made Kerry wonder why they'd split up. Maybe it was because Izzy had a wandering eye. Kerry hadn't missed the less than subtle compliment she'd paid her, but she'd paid no mind to it because as attractive as Izzy was, she wasn't Alice. Nobody was, Kerry realised with a catch in her heart.

Hearing the front door close downstairs, Kerry's pulse raced. Izzy had probably gone which meant Alice would be alone. Checking everything with Carol was OK, Kerry made her way downstairs in search of Alice. She found her in the living room, her head resting back against the sofa, a tumbler with dark liquid in her hand.

'You OK?' Kerry asked, checking to see if she was awake or just resting her eyes.

It was a few seconds before Alice removed her hands from her face and glanced up. This time though there was no hint of desire, in fact, if Kerry wasn't wrong, she seemed angry. *Have I done something wrong?* Kerry searched her brain and couldn't come up with one scenario in which she could have angered Alice. In which case, it could only boil down to one thing. She'd had an argument with Izzy. Kerry's heart sank. If that was the case and Alice was upset, that meant she must still have feelings for her.

It was only then Kerry realised it was a blessing in disguise that Carol only needed her for another week. She wouldn't have been able to bear coming into work if Alice and Izzy were together. Not that she begrudged either woman their happiness, but she knew it would mess with her head. For the past five years, she'd lived a muted silence and it wasn't something that she wanted long term.

'Actually, I'm not,' Alice finally said, putting her glass on the coffee table and standing.

'If you want to talk, I'm—'

'Did you know?' Alice demanded.

Even in anger, Alice looked captivating and Kerry couldn't help but wonder how that anger would translate into the bedroom. Was she a domineering lover? *STOP IT!!! There's something obviously wrong with her but all you can think about is sex!*

'Know what?'

Alice arched an eyebrow, something Kerry had never seen her do before.

'That my mum is going to France?'

'Oh that?' The tension in Kerry's shoulders relaxed. 'Yes, and I think it's great that she has the confidence to travel. Many people, once they've had a stroke, lose their independence and become hermits in their home.'

'That's all I needed to know.' Alice grabbed her

jacket and without bothering to put it on, strode past Kerry and headed down the hallway.

'See you tomorrow.'

Kerry opened her mouth to respond but shut it promptly, not quite understanding why Alice seemed angry at her about her mother's travel plans. Kerry could do nothing but stare at Alice's retreating figure until she disappeared behind the front door. All thoughts of communication gone with her.

This is why Kerry had remained single since Sarah's death, and would be for the foreseeable future.

After seeing Alice's erratic behaviour, it made Kerry wonder if she'd had a lucky escape.

***

The mighty sound of glass smashing in the kitchen, followed by a heavy object crashing on the floor, jolted Kerry from her thoughts. High on adrenaline, her first instinct and utmost concern was Carol. Leaping out of her seat, Kerry moved stealthily along the hallway, calling the police as she did so. In a calm, low steady voice she whispered to the police operator that something had been thrown through the window and she didn't know if the perpetrator was still outside the premises.

The advice – Leave the property immediately.

She would follow his authoritative order only once she had Carol safely beside her.

Seeing no threat on the lower level, Kerry

mounted the steps two at a time, reaching Carol's room breathless. She paused at the door for a few seconds to calm her nerves. Causing Carol alarm would only exacerbate the situation. She had to do this in an orderly manner.

Slowly opening the door, Kerry tiptoed over to Carol's bed and turned the bedside lamp on.

'Carol,' she spoke softly, though her breathing was heavy.

No response.

'Carol.' She rested her hand on Carol's shoulder, inhaling slowly to force her body to relax. It was then she smelt the strong odour of alcohol.

Great!

Izzy must have given it to her and now she'd passed out. She would have to keep a closer eye on her from now on to ensure it didn't happen again.

Carol stirred slightly before opening her eyes.

'Carol, there's nothing to worry about but I need you to come downstairs with me.'

Carol groaned in frustration. 'What time is it?'

'Not late. Please, come on, let me help you up.'

Police sirens wailed in the near distance, getting closer by the second. As though handling a fragile ornament, Kerry helped Carol out of bed and into a thick woolly dressing gown and slippers then led her slowly downstairs and into a wheelchair, eyes alert for any unexpected appearances.

Heart still racing, Kerry wheeled Carol safely outside by which time two police cars had arrived on the scene and officers surrounded the property, torches blazing.

'What's going on?' Carol asked in confusion.

'Someone smashed a window, and I called the police. Don't worry, you're safe.'

Carol laughed as she looked at Kerry's hands. 'I think you're the one who's worried. Look, you're shaking like a leaf.'

Kerry glanced down at her white knuckles gripping Carol's chair. It wasn't so much fear, but more concern that Carol was protected.

'Carol, are you OK?' Mary asked as she neared, her hair in rollers and wearing a nightgown.

Kerry watched in disbelief as Carol's demeanour quickly changed from nonchalant to that of being fearful. 'Oh, it's awful, Mary. Someone broke in, they are after me!'

Mary put a protective arm around Carol's shoulder. 'Come on. You're going to stay at mine tonight.'

A police officer stood nearby, stepped forward and said to Mary, 'That's a good idea.'

Chatter came through on his radio and he turned away from the women, moving the radio near to his ear. He then turned back to them.

'A lad's been caught throwing a brick through another window a few streets away. He's admitted the damage caused here. He's had a few too many beers. He'll be sleeping his hangover off in the cells.'

'Good, he could've put the poor woman back in hospital.' Mary turned to Kerry. 'You'd better get in touch with Alice so she can get the window fixed.'

'Of course,' Kerry said. 'I'll call her now. I'll drop over a few of your things, Carol.'

Carol gave a weak nod then let herself be wheeled away by Mary.

'Can you drop by the station tomorrow and make a statement?'

'Sure, I'll come first thing,' Kerry said.

Kerry went back into the house, gathered Carol's toiletries and a dressing gown then handed them over to Mary at her door. Apparently, Carol was having a night cap to help her cope with the shock.

On her way back to Carol's house, Kerry's first call to Alice went unanswered, leading her to imagine all sorts of things. Alice in bed with Izzy, spooning her, trailing the nape of her neck with soft kisses. She felt physically heartbroken at the thought. Kerry redialled and Alice picked up immediately.

'Is something wrong? I was in the bathroom.'

'Everything's fine. There was an attempted break in. The police are here—'

'I'm on my way.'

The phone went dead before Kerry could tell her it wasn't necessary.

By the time Alice arrived, Kerry had cleaned up the shards of glass and made a makeshift window with a board she'd found in a cupboard. Turning around when she heard Alice come in, Kerry was shocked to see how tired Alice looked.

'You really shouldn't have come. The police had it

under control.'

'I was worried… about you both.'

Kerry liked that and smiled at her as she sat on the edge of the sofa. 'Your mum's staying at Mary's for the night.'

Alice eyed the broken window. 'Good job. I'll call the window people in to repair it in the morning.'

Alice leant against the door frame, crossing one ankle over the other. 'I'm sorry about earlier. I was upset that no one told me my mum was going away.'

'I'd only found out minutes earlier. I was as shocked as you.'

'So you didn't know?' Alice said, shaking her head.

'Of course not. I would've mentioned it if I did.'

So that's why she behaved the way she did. Alice thought I was keeping secrets from her. It all made sense now and Kerry felt ashamed at misjudging her.

'I would've spoken to you about it straight away.'

'I know. I'm sorry.' Alice pushed herself to her feet. 'Can I get you a drink? My way of apologising?'

The genuine sorrow in Alice's eyes didn't afford Kerry much choice other than to say yes. If she went home, she'd only be up all night.

'Sure.'

'Great, what'll it be. Gin—'

'I'm not much of a drinker to be honest. Tea will be fine.'

'Tea it is.' Alice grinned.

They moved into the kitchen and Alice put the kettle on before pouring herself a gin and tonic. She took a mouthful before tipping it down the sink.

'I think it's a bit too late, even for me, to start drinking,' Alice said, before letting out a long yawn.

'Forget about the tea. Since I'm no longer on the clock, I'm gonna make a move.' Kerry got to her feet. 'Why don't you go to bed and get some sleep.'

'Only if you join me.'

'Sorry! I don't mean it like that,' Alice added quickly in response to Kerry's wide-eyed expression. She gestured to the sound of the downpour of rain that had started in the last few minutes. 'It's too late to drive home in these conditions. It's a king-sized bed, so plenty of room.'

'I don't have anything to wear.'

'Don't worry, we can build a wall down the middle if you like. A big wall.'

Kerry laughed at the thought of it. 'Sure, as long as you don't snore.'

Now it was Alice's turn to laugh. 'Me snore? Never.'

'I believe you.'

Kerry followed Alice upstairs, switching off the lights in the process.

She was going to sleep with her boss.

Hypothetically anyway.

Chapter Twenty

The plan had always been to go back home after making sure her mother was safe, but like most things lately, that plan seemed to have gone awry.

Alice drifted off to sleep while listening to Kerry's breathing even out and become shallower. As she'd promised, Alice had constructed a wall of pillows right down the middle of the mattress, sure it would remain securely in place, but of course, it hadn't. Somehow, through the night, the wall collapsed and now lay in ruins across the bed. Alice had woken up with her head resting on Kerry's naked shoulder, Kerry's erect nipple straining against her cotton vest, merely inches from Alice's mouth.

As gently as she could, Alice tried to ease herself away. She was in bed with the nurse who was caring for her mother. Despite Alice's feelings, she hadn't hired Kerry in order to seduce her.

Hence the furtive escape.

Alice had to admit that her nipple did look rather delicious to say the least. The temptation to pull Kerry's top to the side and slip it between her teeth…

Stop it!

The crisp white sheet slid off Kerry's back as Alice gently removed her head from Kerry's shoulder and onto the pillow. The silver glow of moonlight highlighted Kerry's flawless physique. Her skin still bore the remnants of a summer tan.

Goosepimples erupted on Alice's arms as she lay transfixed at the sight. Tucked away at the back of her mind was the desire to reach out and touch Kerry, to kiss her, to…

Forget about it, this can't go anywhere.

Alice turned over, again keeping her movements as slow as she could possibly make them to avoid jostling and waking Kerry. As soon as Alice lay on her side, a soft hand touched her shoulder, and she knew, one way or another, that she was in big trouble.

'I'm sorry,' Alice whispered, looking at Kerry over her shoulder.

'What for?' Kerry asked.

'For… for…'

'You haven't done anything, have you?'

'No! Of course not. But I—'

Kerry gently pulled Alice onto her back and shifted up onto one elbow. 'In that case, don't say another word. If you do, I'll be forced to shut you up… with a kiss.'

Alice couldn't help herself. The excitement started to rise inside her.

'But I'm—'

Nothing could have prepared Alice for the explosion of Kerry's kiss as Kerry cut short her protest by possessing her mouth, their tongues dancing together in a silent melody.

Alice let out a little groan at the schism of electricity Kerry's touch sent through her. As though transported on a runaway train, her emotions whirled and skidded as her thoughts spun out of control. The timing was so wrong. Kerry deserved to know what she was letting herself in for before things went any further.

Alice pulled away. 'Kerry. We shouldn't.'

'Why?' Kerry whispered softly as she removed her top in one swift movement. 'We're both adults.'

Kerry's fingers unbuttoned Alice's shirt and pushed it back as her lips seared a path down Alice's neck to her shoulders, blazing a trail of fire across her skin to Alice's breast, Kerry's warm mouth sucking her taut nipples, rousing an ache between Alice's legs.

Blood pounded between her ears as she floundered in an agonising maelstrom of indecision. How far should Alice let things go before she told Kerry the truth about her plans to leave the UK? Did she even need to? With desire radiating through Alice's body, she shook off her negative train of thoughts. *Now really isn't the time to have a conversation about the future.*

The last traces of resistance disappeared as she stroked a finger across Kerry's cheek, tipping her chin up so their eyes met. 'You're so beautiful.'

Removing her clothes, Alice slowly slid on top of Kerry, strategically placing her leg between her inviting thighs.

Dropping on one elbow, her mouth moved to Kerry's ear. 'Are you sure you want to do this?'

Kerry tilted her head back, exposing her neck for Alice to trail with teasing kisses along every inch of her skin.

'What are we doing?'

A soft gasp escaped Kerry's lips as she wiggled out of her underwear.

The question Alice had posed was moot now. Alice couldn't stop if she wanted to. The momentum had begun, and it would take more than wild horses to hold her back.

Kerry drew Alice's head up, her lips recapturing Alice's again, only this time more demanding. Her nails dug into Alice's buttocks, clasping Alice tightly against her.

The sensual heat of Kerry's naked skin, the feel of her hot liquid leaving a trail against Alice's leg, exalted her. To know that Kerry was just as turned on gave Alice victorious pleasure.

I can't believe this is happening.

The friction between Alice's legs became more intense as Kerry arched her back, giving herself to Alice as their breathing became heavier together, their urges more frantic. Two bodies united in a moment of passion.

Alice squeezed her eyes shut tightly, the sheer intensity of emotion overwhelming her.

She would have liked to have stayed in this moment forever… soaring… as their bodies merged into one.

Alice's hand found Kerry's centre, circling her clit with the tip of her finger.

Kerry groaned in response, their kiss urgent and exploratory as Alice slid her fingers inside her.

'You're so wet,' Alice whispered, her fingers and lips continuing their hungry search of her as Kerry widened her legs, allowing Alice to increase the rhythm of her fingers.

Soft groans escaped Kerry's lips as Alice thrust deeper inside of her with more urgency each time.

Kerry writhed uncontrollably beneath Alice's touch as her body reacted to the stimulation.

The more Kerry's breath came in long surrendering groans, the harder Alice fucked her. Kerry's muscles contracted around her fingers and Alice knew it wouldn't be long before Kerry climaxed.

Sliding down in between her legs, Alice feather-touched Kerry with the tip of her tongue, slowly increasing the pressure as she alternated between sucking and flicking her engorged clit.

Kerry's body tightened before breaking out in a crescendo of spasms.

'Oh my God,' Kerry cried out breathlessly. She gripped Alice's head between her hands as she came hard from her ministrations.

Slowly, Kerry's body eased its trembling and Alice exhaled a deep breath as she slid up the bed, kissing every inch of Kerry's body as she did.

Reaching Kerry's mouth, Alice traced the fullness of her lips with her tongue before parting them and kissing her gently, allowing Kerry to taste her own juices before lying down beside her.

Kerry turned to Alice and ran her fingers through her hair.

'I can't move.' Kerry lifted her head slightly off the pillow. 'For now. Give me a few seconds.'

'Seconds?' Alice laughed.

'OK, a couple of minutes. I feel like I've run a marathon.' Kerry paused, before adding, 'Twice.'

Chapter Twenty-One

Kerry was exhausted. She had slept a few hours with Alice snuggled securely in her arms, but it was clearly not enough for her. Last night was wild. She had needed her, needed Alice to touch every part of her body in every possible way, and told her that over and over again.

Alice stirred against her. Gazing down, she looked even more radiant under the morning light.

Kerry looked over at the digital clock – 7 a.m.

Should she get up and get dressed in case Carol returned early? Probably. It wouldn't look good if she came home and found them in bed together.

As much as she wanted to remain where she was, Kerry moved slowly, trying to remove Alice's arm from where it lay on her stomach, but failed as Alice opened her eyes, blinking a few times before focusing on Kerry.

'Good morning…' Alice said sleepily.

'Morning,' Kerry replied, dropping a kiss on her forehead. Then her eyes. Her nose. Her mouth.

Alice locked her hands around Kerry's neck as their kiss deepened. 'I've always fantasised about sleeping with a nurse.'

Although Alice stared unblinkingly into her eyes, Kerry couldn't tell if she was being serious or not. Despite this, she decided to play along anyway.

'And did it live up to your expectations?'

Alice looked thoughtful for a few seconds then

grinned lazily. 'Hmm, to be honest, there was one thing that let the whole experience down.'

'And what was that?'

Alice drew Kerry's hand between her legs. 'You know when you were doing…'

'This?'

Alice widened her legs as Kerry pushed two fingers deep inside her.

Thoughts of Carol's return now a distant memory, Kerry absorbed Alice's moans into her mouth, kissing her as she thrust her fingers into her wetness over and over.

'Mmm, that feels so good.'

Pressure built between Kerry's own legs as she entwined them with Alice's firm thigh and rubbed her clit gently against it, excitement flooding her veins.

Kerry didn't want to seem too eager for yet another orgasm, but she couldn't help herself as she increased the pressure against Alice's leg, momentarily forgetting that it was Alice who was supposed to be the focus of her attention.

It had been years since she'd been touched or had touched anyone else, and now desire had arisen in her again, it refused to die down.

Kerry tucked her body into the curve of her own and continued to grind against her. There was nothing more enticing than seeing Alice pinned beneath her, their hot juices mixing together as their clits rubbed against each other in a high tempo rhythmic dance.

Kerry couldn't silence her scream of pleasure as

the pressure in her swollen clit ached, wanting fast relief as she rubbed faster and harder until it became too sensitive to do so.

'Orgasm thief,' Alice said, laughing as she buried her hands in Kerry's hair.

'I'm so sorry. I couldn't help myself,' Kerry said, joining in with her laughter as she rolled breathlessly onto her back.

'I forgive you… just this once.'

'That makes me feel a whole lot better.'

Alice rested her head on the palm of her hand and observed her for a while.

Feeling as if Alice could see right into her soul, Kerry edged away, slightly uncomfortable under her gaze. Could Alice sense there was something different about her?

'Why are you staring at me like that?' Kerry asked, finally unable to bear the intensity.

'Because you're beautiful and I like looking at you. As well as touching you.' Alice reached out and stroked her cheek gently.

The intimacy of the moment proved too much for Kerry, it excited her and scared her at the same time. How much more of a warning sign that she'd done the wrong thing by not telling Alice she might be pregnant?

This isn't right.

Guilt forced itself to the forefront of her mind. *I should have told her the truth.*

All Kerry knew right then was that she needed to put a little distance between them. She quickly kissed

          Jade Winters

the back of Alice's hand and climbed out of bed, picking up a robe that lay on an old wicker chair nearby.

'I'm going to make some coffee. Do you want some?' Kerry said, chancing a look into Alice's eyes.

Alice smiled. 'There's something you're not telling me, Kerry, I can see that, but yes, coffee would be lovely, and don't worry about your little secret. I'm sure you'll tell me in your own time.'

Kerry needed to remain calm and get her emotions under control.

'Can I borrow this dressing gown?' Kerry asked, completely ignoring Alice's comment.

'Sure. I'll get dressed and be down in a few moments.'

Kerry fled before she changed her mind.

Tying a knot in the cord as she trotted down the stairs, Kerry headed straight to the kitchen and, fighting the desire to burst into tears, managed to get the coffee pot working and herself under control. By the time Alice appeared, Kerry was retrieving the butter and conserves from the fridge when the doorbell rang.

'Who's that at this time of the morning? I've just spoken to Mary, Mum's still in bed,' Alice said as she slumped down in a chair at the dining table and breathed in the aroma of the coffee. 'Would you mind getting it? You've exhausted me.'

Kerry closed the fridge door, dropped the stuff she had picked up on the table, cinched the belt of the dressing gown around her waist, and headed to the door.

It rang again before she got there.

'Hang on a minute,' Kerry said as she opened the door.

'Oh. Sorry, I didn't mean to wake you.' Izzy looked Kerry up and down.

'You didn't, we were up, I mean I was—'

'Tending to both mother and daughter by the looks of things,' Izzy said dryly.

Kerry tried her level best not to bite at the not-so-subtle jibes coming from Izzy's direction.

Izzy looked at her in distaste before brushing past her. 'Mmm, is that coffee I smell, and toast? I'm starving.'

Izzy headed straight for the kitchen, leaving a fuming Kerry to trail after her in her wake.

Kerry saw Alice's face fall upon seeing Izzy. She was clearly mortified at her sudden appearance.

Without asking, Izzy picked up Kerry's coffee and took a sip.

Kerry watched her with rising anger. An emotion she rarely felt.

'God this is so good,' Izzy said, sinking into the chair Kerry was hoping to sit in. 'I always said your mum had the best coffee, and I wasn't wrong.'

Alice was still staring at Izzy, and hadn't said a word either. Until now.

'What are you doing here so early?' Alice asked.

Izzy feigned innocence as she casually looked at her watch.

'Oh, I didn't realise it wasn't even eight. My body

clock is all over the place at the moment.' Izzy took another sip of coffee. 'To be honest, I wasn't expecting to see you here.'

'I bet you weren't,' Alice said pointedly. 'So who were you expecting to see?'

Izzy's eyes wandered guiltily to her coffee cup. 'I thought your mum would like a day out. You know, different scenery.'

'At seven in the morning?' Kerry broke in before she could stop herself.

'Like I said, I thought it was later than that.' Izzy leant over and grabbed a piece of toast, taking a large bite out of it. 'Seeing as I'm here, I might as well wait until she wakes up.'

Rage suffused Kerry's cheeks. She couldn't put into words how she was feeling right then. All she knew was that she was angry, but she didn't know if it was because of Izzy's blatant lies or because Izzy had ruined what would have been a nice breakfast with Alice.

In the end, Kerry told herself to keep her emotions in check. She wanted nothing to do with the games Izzy was playing. If that was their thing, it was best they were left alone to get on with it.

'I've got to stop by the hospital to sign some forms so I'm going to make a move if that's OK?' Kerry said, directing the question to Alice.

Alice looked at her in confusion. 'Aren't you going to eat?'

'I'll grab something on my way home.'

Alice rose from her seat as Kerry went to leave,

but Kerry stopped her with a hand gesture as she passed her. 'Don't worry, I'll see myself out, don't let the food go cold.'

'We won't.' Izzy grinned as she polished off the last piece of toast.

When she left the house minutes later, Kerry didn't bother looking back to see if Alice was watching her from one of the windows, as she had done a few times now, always covering it up with a jaunty wave goodbye.

What was she doing alone in the house with Izzy now?

It was that thought occupying her mind on her journey home. Not the amazing hot sex she'd had with Alice.

Chapter Twenty-Two

The day Emily had been dreading was now upon her. Throughout the hour's drive, she'd given herself a stern self-talk of what not to say and how to behave. She was not to interrupt, be defensive, raise her voice, curse or say anything derogatory about her father. Instead, she was to sit and listen politely, smile when it was appropriate and leave a lasting impression of being the woman Arnold thought she was – one of sweetness and light. Under no circumstances could she let him ruin her book deal.

It took Arnold several minutes to answer the door, during which time she had settled the rage that dwelt within. The fact that she even had to come and listen to his garbage made her want to scream. Her father still had some control over her. Even from the grave.

Arnold gave her a warm welcome even though their last encounter hadn't exactly ended on friendly terms. She followed him into his tiny living room with its small electric fire, outdated furniture and rows and rows of photographs hung on the faded blue walls. It was such a far cry from his younger days when he was Jack the lad with women falling at his feet. Fast cars and fast money, everything a man could want. Yet now, sadly, he was just a lonely old man with only memories for company.

'I didn't think I'd see you again.' Arnold coughed into a hanky that looked like it hadn't been washed in a while.

Emily fought against her natural instinct to have compassion for him. Instead, she switched her emotions off. Something she could do at a drop of a hat whenever she thought about her father.

'It was unfair of me not to hear you out the other day. I didn't mean to be so rude.'

'No need to apologise, Lee.'

Grr why is he using my nickname?

'There is, Arnold, and I'm sorry.' She refrained from letting out the sigh that was caught in her throat. 'So what was it you had to tell me?'

'Can I get you something to drink first? A cup of tea?'

'I'm good. I stopped at a drive through on the way.'

'Never thought I'd see something like that in my day – pulling up next to a window to get a hot drink, and the prices they charge too. Madness.'

Emily nodded in agreement. So far so good. She was reacting as planned.

'I take it you want to hear the truth now?'

'Yes, Arnold, that's correct.' *Easy!* It wasn't as easy as that when the tension in her shoulders slowly crept up her neck.

'I knew you'd come 'round. The Emily I remember would never sully a good man's name.'

Now Emily really did have to bite her tongue, forcing herself to swallow the words she would have let rip under normal circumstances. How dare he make such a statement? He wasn't the one on the receiving end of her dad's neglect and emotional abuse. She was. Alice was.

Arnold coughed again and this time specks of red stained the discoloured cloth. Noticing her sudden interest, Arnold quickly stuffed the hanky into his pocket.

'Arnold, I know you and my dad were as thick as thieves—'

He nodded fondly. 'We were and that's why I want to tell you the truth.'

'Go on then… what's the truth?'

Arnold leant forward, removing his glasses from his face. He stared into her eyes with such ferocity she thought he was going to start shouting any minute. Instead, when he spoke, his tone was soft, gentle.

'That everything your mother told you about your dad was a lie.'

Chapter Twenty-Three

Carol returned shortly after Kerry left, and Alice helped her to her room to change before joining Izzy again in the kitchen. If Carol hadn't been in the house, Alice wouldn't have remained so civil when inside she was boiling with fury. Izzy had no right to be so dismissive of Kerry.

'Did you have to be so rude?'

Alice immediately felt a softening in her emotions. The reason? Just thinking Kerry's name. Just the thought of her felt like a soothing balm. No, she wouldn't let Izzy spoil her day or her memories. It was probably what she wanted.

'I wasn't rude, Al, if anything I was more than polite, which is more than can be said for you two. Seriously, shagging in your mum's house like a pair of horny teenagers? I expected better of you?'

Alice was literally lost for words. Izzy expected better of her?! *Is she taking the piss?*

Before Alice could come out with a retort, Izzy carried on, she was far from finished.

'Not to mention how unprofessional Kerry is. Having sex while on duty. I mean, isn't that a sackable offence?'

Alice didn't like the way Izzy was looking at her. Not one little bit. She'd seen that vindictive expression on her face many times before.

'Kerry was not on duty, as you put it, and mum wasn't in the house, so no she wasn't being unprofessional. I swear, Izzy, I hope you're not thinking of doing anything stupid.'

Izzy feigned innocence. 'What?'

'Don't act dumb. You know exactly what I mean.'

'Well that all depends, doesn't it?'

'Meaning?' Alice asked, wondering what on earth Izzy could want from her. Wasn't it enough that she'd betrayed her?

'Fire her.'

Alice cocked her head, unsure she'd heard Izzy correctly.

'What did you say?' Alice dropped the remains of her toast on her plate.

'You heard me. I said fire her.' Izzy sat back nonchalantly. 'If you do, I won't report her.'

'Report her for what? She hasn't done anything wrong.'

'Somehow, I don't think her boss would agree.'

'Are you blackmailing me?'

Izzy's expression said it all.

Appalled, Alice jumped to her feet and stood in front of her. 'Tell me you're joking?'

Izzy looked up at her. Eyes narrowed so Alice could barely see the whites of her eyes.

'Nope. I'm deadly serious. Despite what you think of me, Alice, I do actually have some values. Just imagine, if she's sleeping with the daughter of one client, how many other people is she doing it with?'

Alice rolled her eyes, unable to believe the tripe coming out of Izzy's mouth, but the truth was that Izzy would follow through on her threats. She was that vindictive. Another red flag Alice had blissfully ignored during their time together.

Alice sighed in exasperation. What the hell was she going to do? This was all her fault. She should never have suggested sleeping in the same bed together.

That was mistake number one.

Mistake number two was not being able to control herself. Something that she was normally very good at, but when it had come down to Kerry, her self-control had gone out the window.

'I don't believe this,' Alice muttered as she turned her back to Izzy.

'It wouldn't have worked anyway,' Izzy said lightly, her tone full of self-confidence, 'rebound relationships never do.'

Alice spun around, enraged. 'Rebound? You think this is about you?'

'Isn't it?'

'Not in a million fucking years,' Alice said. 'You have nothing on Kerry. Nothing!'

'Well, there's the fact I know she slept with you. I'd say I've got quite a lot on her, wouldn't you?'

'Alice!' Carol shouted from the top of the stairs.

Izzy stood. 'Ah Carol, I'll come and help you.'

Izzy's tone suddenly changed from one of hostility to one of joviality in a split second.

'Good to see you looking refreshed,' Izzy said as

she eased Carol down the stairs and into the wheelchair.

Carol eyed them both suspiciously as Izzy wheeled her into the kitchen. 'You two trying to wake the whole neighbourhood?'

Izzy feigned innocence again. Something Alice realised she was a master at.

'Of course not. We were just discussing you. I thought it would be a good idea to take you out for the day. Get your eyes away from these boring four walls, but your daughter here thinks it'll be too much for you.'

'She would. She's been keeping me prisoner in my own home.'

Izzy grinned. 'Exactly what I said. So what d'you say. You fancy coming out with me?'

'Is my name Carol? Give me fifteen minutes to put my face on. No, make that five.'

Alice turned to Carol pleadingly. 'Mum, you're not well—'

'That's enough, Alice. If it was up to you, I'd never leave my bed—'

'That's not true.'

'Yes, it is. I think Izzy is right about you being here so much. You're nothing but a hindrance to my recovery.'

Alice frowned. 'How can you say such a thing? I care about you.'

'Do you? Or is it about controlling me?'

'What the,' Alice stopped abruptly before the swear word left her mouth. That was one thing her mother would never tolerate in the house after their father left. Alice knew it was because their father did nothing but yell expletives at her mother, especially when he was drunk. At those times, every other word began with an F. 'Where the hell is all this coming from? What crap have you been feeding my mother, Izzy?'

Izzy smirked. 'Carol's a grown woman. She can make decisions for herself.'

'That's right. Sometimes I think you forget who the mother is in this relationship.'

Alice stood stunned. She was at a loss what to say. Stuck in the middle of two foes, she decided to let them get on with it. If her mother wanted to undo all the good she'd achieved up until now that was her business. Alice was washing her hands of the whole situation.

Maybe Emily had been right all along. It was best just to not get involved.

Not that she'd ever tell Emily that.

It took a whole ten minutes for Alice to get her stuff together and leave the toxicity of her mother's house. She could barely breathe it was so suffocating.

***

Alice tried calling Kerry on and off for the past hour, but the calls went straight to voicemail. She remembered Kerry mentioning her plan to pop into the hospital, so Alice decided to go in search of her on the off chance she was still there.

Finding the ward Kerry worked on proved harder than she'd imagined. The hospital was not only like a maze, but it seemed that every other door was one ward or another. The receptionist at the entrance of the hospital hadn't been much help. Obviously stressed out by the large queue backing up behind her, she barked at Alice, informing her she was not at liberty to tell the public the whereabouts of staff members. So Alice had started the daunting task of searching for Kerry herself.

Ward by ward Alice pressed on the buzzer asking for Nurse Kerry Miller, and each reply that came back said the same thing, 'Kerry doesn't work on this ward'.

Alice was determined not to give up though. She had to talk to her before Kerry returned to her mother's that evening.

Alice pressed yet another buzzer. 'Hello?'

'I'm looking for Nurse Kerry Miller.'

Waiting for the familiar response, Alice readied herself to move on. Instead, her ears pricked up when she heard the voice say, 'One moment.'

Alice waited for the next few minutes in anticipation. Preparing herself for the bad news she was going to impart. What choice did she have? If she didn't let Kerry go from her position as her mother's carer, she could lose her job at the hospital.

The door to the ward opened and a blonde woman in a blue uniform stepped out. Alice was disappointed to see it wasn't Kerry.

'You lookin' for Kerry?'

Alice nodded. The woman spoke Kerry's name with familiarity, it was obvious she knew her.

'My name's Alice. Kerry looks after my mum.'

A look of recognition sparked in the woman's eyes.

'You hired her from the care agency.' It was a statement not a question.

'Yes, is she here?'

''Fraid not, she's been and gone.'

'Damn,' Alice said under her breath.

'Is everything OK?' The nurse asked. 'Is it urgent?'

Alice nodded. It wasn't a matter of life or death, but it was close enough. Kerry could be out of a job pretty soon. 'I've been trying to get hold of her on her mobile, but it's switched off.'

The nurse briefly looked over her shoulder, before removing her mobile phone from her pocket. 'I'll give her a ring on her landline, one min.'

The relief that shot through Alice was enough to make her sink to the floor. The sheer tension Alice carried on her shoulders no longer weighed her down.

'Gotta be quick, Kerry, you know what the witch is like,' the nurse said into the phone.

She passed the phone over to Alice who gave her a grateful smile.

'Kerry?'

'Is everything all right?'

'We need to talk, can we meet?'

'Now? I've barely had any sleep.'

Alice turned away from the nurse and walked to the other side of the corridor. She spoke in hushed tones.

'We've got a problem.'

'What kind of problem?'

'It's Izzy.'

'Shit. I knew it.'

'Can you come and meet me?'

'Ask Debbie to tell you where Bean's café is. I'll meet you there in twenty minutes. Try not to worry, we'll sort this out'

'I know we will.'

Though she could tell Kerry was trying to put a positive spin on things, Alice knew there was no way out of this mess.

The only thing she could do was let Kerry go.

Chapter Twenty-Four

The drive on the motorway had been a nightmare. Traffic clogged up every fifteen minutes for absolutely no reason. Miles of roadworks with not a soul to be seen actually working. Services selling worse than mediocre food at gourmet prices. All of those minor annoyances had soured her mood and left her with a pounding headache by the time Emily reached Maggie's house.

She pulled up outside and switched off the car, hearing only the metallic click of the engine as it began to cool after its long journey.

Emily unwrapped a chocolate bar and took a large chunk between her teeth, chewing the soft toffee centre slowly. She didn't care that the sugar laden treat would cause a spike in her blood sugar levels followed by a sharp drop that would cause her to eat another one, then another one and one after that. It was a downward spiral once she got started which is why she fought to keep sugar out of her diet.

Her leg bounced up and down in the small space her car seat afforded her. The digital clock on the dashboard clicked over to 13:45. She'd been sat in her car for over an hour.

What the hell am I doing here?

Emily tapped her finger against her lip as her gaze focused on the stone path leading up to the small run down detached house, and thought about the many times her father would have walked up that same path, entering his mistress's house instead of his own home.

Now she was expected to do the same and listen to another pack of lies. But what choice did she have? If she didn't, Arnold would follow through with disputing the book she was writing about her father. Controversy was normally considered a good thing in terms of generating publicity for an upcoming book. *For other people's biographies maybe.* Emily reminded herself. *Not my father's.* This was way too close to home, having the family's dirty laundry put on public display before the book was even finished.

Once it was public, they would have all the facts. Not just the select few Arnold envisioned. Even though she asked him time and time again to simply tell her what he deemed the 'truth', he insisted Emily talk to Maggie. That she would be the one who would provide all the answers she was looking for.

That was where Arnold had been wrong. Emily wasn't looking for answers. She knew the truth, and the truth was that she knew exactly who her father was. She didn't need a woman with zero morals to fill her in.

Stuffing the empty chocolate wrapper in her pocket, Emily undid her seat belt.

Time to face the music. The sooner she got this over with, the sooner she could put it all behind her and get back to what was her main priority – finishing her book.

No longer able to prolong her visit, Emily quietened her racing thoughts by inhaling and exhaling. Emily breathed herself into the right headspace where she wasn't overwrought by her emotions, because if she didn't and then walked into Maggie's house, God only knew what she'd end up saying to her. It would be counterproductive which was the last thing Emily wanted.

In and out. No drama.

Emily climbed out of the car, locked it, and made her way to the house.

With a clammy finger, Emily reached for the bell and pressed down on it.

Taking a step back, she waited.

Much sooner than she expected, footsteps sounded near the door, then it swung open to reveal a woman in her late forties, blonde and dressed stylishly in a leather jacket, jeans and knee length boots.

As they came face to face for the first time, the expression on Maggie's face was one that Emily could not interpret. That was until a slow recognition crept into her eyes.

'Emily?' Maggie said in a barely audible voice.

Emily hesitated. Fighting the urge to turn on her heels and flee. This was too real. In her fantasy, she imagined it would be different.

Much different.

That she would be standing at a distance watching as Maggie's coffin was lowered into the ground. Six feet deep. Never to be seen or heard from again. Unable to ruin anyone else's life, the way she had Emily's.

Instead, she stood her ground and nodded.

Maggie smiled and gestured for Emily to follow her which she did.

Maggie led her into the living room. Although only a small space, it was neat and tidy. Curtains matched the puffed-up cushions sat on the three-seater fabric sofa, a small coffee table with an array of lifestyle magazines positioned in front.

The minimalist look.

If they hadn't been sworn enemies, they would have probably got along had they crossed paths under different circumstances.

Her tidiness is probably why dad was attracted to her, Emily reflected as she looked around. To her surprise, despite the many framed photos on the wall, there was only one of her father. One taken of him while performing on stage.

Emily turned away from the picture and looked straight into Maggie's eyes.

'Arnold said you were going to drop by. I didn't believe him.'

'Why?' Emily's voice was terse. She didn't even know why she bothered asking the question. She knew exactly why Maggie wouldn't believe she would turn up. She had ruined her parents' marriage.

'Because,' Maggie spluttered. 'All the… things that have been said about me… aren't true.'

Emily refrained from asking Maggie outright if she thought Emily was a fool.

Even though Emily was estranged from her mother, she would believe her word over Maggie's any day of the week. After all, as bad as her mother was, she hadn't enticed a man away from his family.

Maggie had.

Chapter Twenty-Five

Until the day she died, Kerry knew she would never completely understand human nature. How people could be so vindictive to one another. To get pleasure from intentionally hurting someone. From her own experience, she had witnessed first-hand how those on death's door could remain bitter, even knowing they were merely breaths away from passing on. She had seen it all. Patients with barely enough energy to move, let alone anything else, cursing their family from their death bed. Family members not having the patience to wait until their 'loved ones' had passed over, such was their desperation to return to their normal way of living.

Throughout Sarah's illness, Kerry was grateful for every day. That wasn't her being a martyr. She knew families didn't get on but there was a time for everything, and someone being near death wasn't exactly the appropriate time to bring up past hurts and injustices. That was Kerry's opinion anyway.

That made it even harder for her to understand why Izzy seemed to have it in for her. It wasn't as if Izzy was still in a relationship with Alice. Her animosity towards Kerry would have been understandable if they were, but they weren't, yet Izzy seemed intent on ruining her life.

Navigating her way into the hospital's car park, Kerry parked her car and traversed the path leading to the café.

Cold air whipped her face, causing her to pull the collar of her jacket up further.

The steamed windows of the café made it difficult to see inside, but as soon as Kerry stepped through the threshold, she spotted her. Alice's demeanour revealed her mind was in turmoil. Her head bowed and shoulders slumped, her hands toying relentlessly with a glass saltshaker on the table. Walking towards her, Kerry faintly heard a familiar song playing quietly on the radio about lost love which would have been depressing to hear on any day, not just this one.

As if sensing her presence, Alice looked up as she neared and what Kerry saw in her eyes confirmed the dreaded feeling that had plagued her since they'd spoken on the phone.

Waiting for Alice to speak once Kerry was seated was equivalent to waiting in the doctor's surgery for test results.

Kerry would rather Alice just tell her what decision she'd come to, because it was obvious she'd made one. Kerry hoped her expression didn't reveal the turmoil she was experiencing inside.

Alice undid the band at the back of her head and let her hair fall loosely.

'Just tell me, Alice,' Kerry said after watching Alice comb her fingers through her hair for what seemed like the tenth time.

'OK, I don't know how serious Izzy is but… she's threatened to report you to your agency if I don't fire you.'

This was worse than what Kerry first thought. Stupidly, she'd imagined Izzy giving Alice an ultimatum such as not staying overnight at Carol's, but to threaten to tell Kerry's employer?

That hit below the belt.

Hard.

Kerry's throat constricted and though she wasn't normally one who reached for a drink in times of stress, a double brandy – straight – would have gone down well.

There was a controlled anger in Alice's voice. 'She's trying to imply you've broken the terms of your employment contract.'

Kerry remained silent. There was no counter argument she could come back with. It was true. She'd slept with her client's daughter in the client's house. She would take it on the chin though.

'I'm sorry. I feel horrible about putting you in this position,' Kerry said sincerely.

'I think we were both responsible for what we did.'

It felt odd sitting there with Alice, not talking about the fact that they'd had sex but alluding to it. They were both complicit in a situation that would have been unthinkable to Kerry only hours earlier. What were the chances of Izzy turning up when she did?

Alice was quiet for a few moments and Kerry could tell her mind was racing.

'The only thing I can think of is to come clean and tell your boss you weren't on duty, which technically you weren't. Your shift was over.'

'I don't think my employer would see it quite like that,' Kerry said, a wave of apprehension sweeping through her. Would Esther believe Izzy over her? A woman that she'd never met before versus someone with a stellar reputation. The question was could she take the chance?

'Izzy really has stooped to a new low in my eyes,' Alice said.

'She's like a cat toying with a mouse,' Kerry said quietly, pressing the palms of her hands against her eyes to ease the pressure increasing behind them. She thought of how happy she'd been up until that morning. When everything seemed to be going according to plan. Even the night she'd spent with Alice had made her feel on top of the world. And now? She was like a volcano on the verge of erupting.

'The least I can do is pay you for the rest of the month.'

Kerry stared at her. There was no way she was going to let Alice bail her out. She had put herself in this mess and she was going to have to get herself out of it.

'Don't be silly, you don't owe me anything.'

Alice dropped her gaze to her hands. 'Yes, I do. I should never have encouraged you to get into bed with me.'

'You didn't have a gun to my head, and if I remember correctly, I came willingly.'

They both smiled at the unintended pun.

'I wish there was some way I could magic up a solution and make this all go away.'

A sullen teenage waitress brought over a cup of tea and placed it in front of Kerry without uttering a word. Before Kerry could say thank you, she strode off in the direction of the counter.

Kerry looked at the waitress's retreating figure in confusion. She didn't remember ordering one, or had she? Her mind was in a muddle. Her heart ablaze with rage at the injustice of the world she now found herself in.

'There is one thing we could do,' Alice said, looking up at her now, hope filling her eyes.

'Which is?' Kerry smiled, relieved. There might be a light at the end of the tunnel after all.

Alice leant forward, placing her hand on top of Kerry's. She tried to ignore the warmth that burnt into her skin from Alice's touch and the memories of Alice's hands caressing her in her most intimate places. She failed miserably on both counts.

'We could always present a united front.'

Kerry looked at her, gradually understanding what Alice was alluding to. 'United front? You mean lie and say it never happened.'

'That's exactly what I mean,' Alice said, triumphantly.

Chapter Twenty-Six

Having to involve herself in mind games with Izzy irritated Alice to no end but she couldn't see any other way out. She didn't want to fire Kerry nor go through all the stress of having to find another nurse to care for her mother. They were nearly at the end of the contract anyway so there was no point. Besides, who was to say that if Alice gave into Izzy's threat, she wouldn't use it some time else in the future. No, it was better to cut the poison off at the root before it spread. If Izzy told Carol about their liaison, she would deny it until she was blue in the face.

The café had started to fill now, with groups of students cramming around the few free tables, so she had to keep her voice low.

'We can only do this under two conditions.'

'Go on,' Kerry said cautiously, matching Alice's tone.

'We never, and I mean never admit the truth to anyone, ever! No matter what.'

Kerry nodded in agreement.

'And?' Kerry almost whispered.

Alice glanced away, unable to look Kerry in the eye in case she rejected her offer.

'Go on, what's the second thing?' Kerry pressed.

'You let me take you for lunch.'

Doubt clouded Kerry's eyes.

'Just lunch.' Alice held her hands up in the air. 'I promise, no hanky panky under the table. No emotional talk. Just two women getting to know each other as friends.'

Kerry took a breath and exhaled. 'Sure, why not. I mean, it's not like we can be accused of doing anything in a public place.'

Alice stood, more out of relief than anything else.

'Exactly. Shall we go,' Alice said, gesturing for Kerry to lead the way towards the entrance. 'I know a lovely Italian restaurant ten minutes away.'

'That's great. I happen to love Italian.'

'You do? Me too.'

'Who would have known eh?'

They both laughed as they left the café. A vastly different energy from only minutes previously.

The drive to the restaurant was relaxed and filled with comfortable conversation, just what they needed after the intensity of their previous chat. Alice didn't want to consider what would happen if Izzy called their bluff and reported Kerry. They'd deal with that if it became an issue. For now, Alice wanted to spend a couple of stress-free hours with Kerry, getting to know her better.

Palo, the owner at Ciao, a family run restaurant Alice ate at all the time, gave them a quick rundown on what wasn't available on the menu that day as he led Alice and Kerry to their table at the back of the restaurant where it was secluded and quiet.

It was an intimate space with whitewashed walls

covered with family pictures – Palo at the forefront of all of them with his beaming smile.

They sat down at the small wooden table as they read the menu, acoustic music filling in the comfortable silence.

'Drinks?' Palo said, taking out his little notepad from the pocket of his red waist jacket.

Alice looked to Kerry who said, 'Just water for me thanks. My car's at the hospital.'

'I'll have a small merlot please,' Alice replied.

They both ordered the same dish, sea food pasta, and soon Palo went on his way, leaving them alone.

Alice liked this. For their attention to only be focused on one another. No distractions. Even sitting feet away from Kerry, she so desperately wanted to touch her, even if it was just to hold her hand.

'So have you always wanted to be a nurse?' Alice asked wanting to keep things light-hearted. After the drama they'd had with Izzy, it was better to stick to neutral, safe topics.

'Yes, from a kid. I was always nursing my dolls. Wrapping their arms and legs in bandages.' Kerry laughed as if recalling a long-lost memory. 'Tending to them as if they were real.'

'I must admit, you do have a way with people. I thought my mum would hate being looked after by a stranger, but with you she's not the least bit bothered.'

'I'm glad to hear it.' Kerry reached for a long bread stick in a holder in the middle of the table and snapped it in half. She offered a piece to Alice who took it with a smile. 'And what about you? What were your dreams and aspirations?'

Alice took a bite of the bread stick and chewed thoughtfully for a few seconds. 'To have enough money for a secure peaceful life where I didn't have to rely on anyone.'

Kerry looked at her with widened eyes. 'You felt that way as a kid?'

Alice nodded. 'When my dad left my mum for another woman, we were penniless.'

'Didn't he pay maintenance?'

'Nope, and the worse thing is, they married young, so my mum never had a career. When he walked out, she was pretty lost without him. If it weren't for my sister, I don't know what she would've done.'

Alice still wasn't sure how Emily had come to know about the ins and outs of claiming social security, but she had, and within a few weeks they actually had money to eat every day. She knew it was one of the many things Emily still held against their father. Although Emily had every right to feel that way, Alice didn't. All it had served to do for Alice was to make sure she was never in a position where she relied on someone for her livelihood. Her father's actions actually made her stronger.

Kerry broke off a smaller piece of the bread stick and popped it into her mouth. 'So why the stock market?'

A smile curved Alice's lips at the thought. In the early days, she was at her desk two hours before anyone else and was always the last to leave.

'The buzz of fast money. Nothing in the world could beat it.'

'Could?' Kerry asked, questioningly. 'You don't feel that way about it now?'

'I suppose so. To be honest, I haven't really thought about work that much. I mean, with my mum and her stroke… It was a wake-up call. There's more to life than work.'

Alice was thankful she was finding this out now and not when she burnt out from working eighty-hour weeks. It could have been her in hospital. It was amazing how unexpected incidences could change your whole outlook on life.

'I know this is a sensitive subject so feel free to tell me to mind my own business, but you losing your partner…'

'Sarah,' Kerry corrected her.

Alice smiled apologetically. 'Sorry, Sarah – that must have torn you to bits.'

Kerry hesitated when a waiter appeared with their drinks. As he walked away, Kerry exhaled a deep breath and said, 'There are no words to describe what I went through. Some days I seriously thought I wouldn't make it. All I know is I wouldn't wish it on my worst enemy, not even on someone like Izzy.'

'Who deserves her own place in hell,' Alice said taking a long sip of her wine, welcoming the comforting warmth the alcohol spread throughout her body.

'No comment.'

'So how are you now? Mentally? Is it still tough?'

Kerry shrugged. 'I don't know. I suppose I've become familiar with the new normal. Some days are good, some not. The main thing is I have more good days than bad.'

The waiter returned, this time with their food, and they ate in silence for a while.

'I hope you don't mind me asking you such personal questions. I'm just curious.' Alice wasn't about to say outright that she was fishing to see where things stood between them. There was still some time before she would be leaving the country and it would have been nice to spend that time with Kerry. In and out of bed.

'In that case, anything else you'd like to know?'

'There is actually. Loads,' Alice said, happy to have been given the green light. She dug her fork into a king prawn before savouring it.

'Feel free to ask.'

'OK, do you ever feel lonely?' Stupid question Alice knew, but was that the reason Kerry had slept with her the night before? Could Alice have been anyone? Just a warm body to comfort her?

'Ha! Of course I do. I'm only human.' Kerry forked some pasta into her mouth, speaking again when it was empty. 'I even tried dating a couple of times but couldn't be arsed in the end. Not one of them could compare to Sarah.'

Alice felt an irrational stab of jealousy and was tempted to ask her to define the word date. Did she sleep with them? The thought of Kerry in anyone's arms but her own made Alice feel emotions she had no right feeling.

'Do they have to? I mean compare to Sarah?' Alice finally said instead. She took a mouthful of wine as she waited to hear the answer with a sense of apprehension.

'I don't know if it's so much comparing, it's more like a feeling. You know when you have that connection?'

Alice glanced down as she played with her food. Yes, she knew about connecting with someone all right. She had done so with Kerry and thought Kerry felt the same, but by the sounds of it, she hadn't at all. Alice felt a sense of disappointment. Not that it would have changed her mind and made her stay, but it would have been nice to think that after last night, there was something between them. That it hadn't been a meaningless one-night stand.

'Penny for your thoughts?'

Alice looked up when she realised Kerry had asked her a question.

'Oh sorry, I was thinking about what you said and yeah you're right, it's not easy to find a connection with someone these days.'

'What about you and Izzy? Are things definitely over?'

'Absolutely,' Alice said. 'I wouldn't go back to her if she was the last woman on earth.'

Kerry laughed. 'Thank God she isn't, or we'd all be in trouble.'

Alice was just about to take another sip of wine when her hand froze in mid-air, her body taut and wired.

What the hell are they doing here?

'I think you spoke too soon. We already are.'

Kerry turned around and looked in the direction of Alice's gaze.

'Oh crap,' Kerry said, pushing her plate aside. 'D'you think we should sneak out the back way?'

'Too late, strap yourself in, she's spotted us.' Alice drained her wine glass and steeled herself for the unavoidable encounter with her mother and Izzy. 'We're going to have to act as if we're friends.'

'I hope we aren't just acting?'

Alice's heart skipped a beat. 'Of course not.'

'Good, I'm glad.'

Alice didn't want to be friends with Kerry. She wanted something much, much more, but how could she ask that from a woman whose heart would always belong to someone else?

Alice couldn't compete with a ghost.

Or a memory.

And neither did she want to.

Chapter Twenty-Seven

Just when Kerry thought things were going smoothly, Izzy had to show up and spoil it. *That woman's like a bad penny.* The more she saw of her, the more she couldn't help but wonder what attracted Alice to her. Bar the fact that Izzy was threatening her livelihood with malicious gossip, she was also rather self-centred and full of her own importance. Attributes Kerry herself found a total turn off.

Izzy obviously had the vision of an eagle as she seemed to have spotted them as soon as she'd walked in. Unless the restaurant was a regular haunt of Izzy's, Kerry found it a little strange that she would turn up with Carol at the very exact moment they were there.

Pushing these thoughts aside, Kerry rose as they neared the table. They were obviously going to join them invited or not, which Kerry found slightly rude.

Carol looked a bit unsteady on her feet and the natural instinct in Kerry had her going to Carol's aid.

'Where's your wheelchair? Let me help.'

Carol waved off her help. 'I'm sick of that thing, I don't need it. Anyway, you're not on the clock now.'

'I know but—' Kerry paused long enough to catch a glimpse of Alice whose expression told her to back off. Carol obviously didn't want to be treated like an invalid.

Kerry returned to her seat. Izzy and Carol now sat

at the table with them and Kerry nodded at Izzy in acknowledgement which was point blankly ignored.

'What're you two doing here, socialising out of working hours? Is that allowed?' Carol said while at the same time summoning the waiter with a wave of her hand. He arrived straight away and took her order for a large gin and tonic for both her and Izzy.

'Kerry's your nurse, Mum, not mine,' Alice said in a lowered voice as the waiter moved away from their table. 'What she does in her private life has nothing to do with anyone.'

Kerry could tell Alice was at breaking point already by the way her eyes narrowed as she gave Izzy sideward glances.

'All right, no need to bite my head off,' Carol said.

'I wasn't.' Alice threw her hands up in the air in exasperation. 'Oh, just forget it.'

Kerry desperately wanted to step in and say something to Carol about her disregard for Alice, but all Kerry could do was sit back and watch the woman she had become so fond of suffer in silence.

'Someone got out of the wrong side of bed this morning,' Izzy interjected, a sly grin on her face as she took her drink from the waiter and raised it in Carol's direction before taking a sip.

Oh what I wouldn't do to wipe that look off her face!

'And don't you start!' Alice said, barely able to hide her contempt.

'Ooh touchy, too close to home?' Izzy said.

Carol looked at each of the women. 'Come on you

two, pack it in. You don't behave like this at home, do you?'

'No, we most certainly don't, not anymore, thank God,' Alice said.

Kerry heard the undercurrent in her tone and so did Carol by the look of it. Kerry steeled herself for the oncoming confrontation and hoped Alice would be able to maintain her cool.

'What the hell does that mean?' Carol slammed the glass on the table causing the few customers in the restaurant to turn in their direction.

To Kerry's surprise, Carol didn't seem to notice or care about the attention she was attracting.

'Ignore her.' Izzy picked up the menu and busied herself scanning it.

'No, I won't,' Carol almost barked. 'What did you mean?'

Kerry held her breath.

'You really want to know?' Alice asked, her eyes held a fierce determination Kerry hadn't seen before.

'I wouldn't bloody ask if I didn't.'

'OK, right,' Alice turned her body to face Carol directly. She jabbed a finger in Izzy's direction. 'We are no longer together.'

'What!' Carol was clearly astonished. It seemed that was the last thing she expected to hear.

'And while I'm at it I might as well tell you.'

Kerry braced herself in preparation for what Alice was going to reveal next.

'Out with it then,' Carol barked impatiently.

'I'm unemployed.'

Carol's eyes widened.

'Yep, that's right,' Alice said.

'You were fired I take it?'

'Yes, Mum, I was fired. Happy now?'

Carol shrugged nonchalantly but Kerry didn't miss the look of pleasure in her eyes. A look that quickly turned to disdain.

'I don't know how you got the job in the first place if I'm honest,' Carol said.

'And why's that?'

From Alice's resigned tone it was obvious the two women were familiar at playing this dance with one another.

'Because you could never manage your own money, let alone anyone else's,' Carol said. 'Imagine, all those important people putting their money in the hands of someone who can't even balance a cheque book.'

Kerry sat there aghast. She couldn't believe what she was hearing. Words that shouldn't come from a stranger, let alone your own mother. She dreaded to think of the messages Carol rained down on Alice as a child.

It was surprising to see that Alice had turned out emotionally stable.

I would rather cut my tongue out than speak to my own child like that.

'It's just as well someone did have faith in me then, isn't it? Besides, it doesn't matter. None of it does,' Alice ploughed on, ignoring the steely stare she was getting from Carol. 'Everything's turned out to be a blessing in disguise.'

Phew, so she wasn't going to come clean about their little rendezvous after all.

'And why's that,' Izzy asked, clearly pissed off she even had to ask.

'Because…'

Kerry noted how unsure Alice looked now. The tension around the table grew palpable as they all seemed to wait with bated breath as to the next bombshell Alice was going to drop. Even Kerry couldn't imagine what it would be.

Alice looked at her mother directly than slowly moved onto Kerry.

'I'm leaving to go on a 'round the world trip. I'll be gone a year. Maybe longer.'

There was a stunned silence. Kerry's mouth wouldn't move. What could she say? Congratulations? You walked into my heart and are going to leave without so much as a second glance? They'd had sex. Simple as that. Alice was under no obligation towards her. Yet it still hurt – bad. Why did it cause so much pain to know that Alice wasn't planning on creating a life with her, she wanted to start a brand new one? One without baggage and emotional drama. Not that she blamed her, but that didn't mean the news didn't shoot straight through her heart.

'When were you planning on telling me?' Carol said.

Kerry saw that Carol was struggling to look at Alice directly. Was she scared that Alice would see the pure hatred in her eyes?

'Soon… I don't know.' Alice shrugged. 'When you got back on your feet I suppose.'

'And if I didn't?' Carol gave a hard hacking cough.

'Please, let's not play the what if game. The great news is that you're feeling better. You're even well enough to go to see your sister in France.'

Kerry's anger sparked. She couldn't bear the animosity around the table any longer and although she might get fired for crossing the boundary, she wasn't going to sit there and be a party to what boiled down to bullying. If she had to wait tables to save money for the baby so be it.

'For what it's worth, I think that's amazing, Alice. Congratulations. What a fantastic opportunity. It's something a lot of people could only wish for in their lifetime.'

Kerry could see tears well in Alice's eyes and it pained her heart.

'I take it your sister knows about your plans?' The bitterness in Carol's voice was plain to hear.

'Actually, she doesn't. This is the first time I'm telling anyone.'

'You say that like we should feel privileged,' Izzy said. 'You're so selfish, d'you know that? Springing something like this on your poor mum when she's still not out of the woods.'

'What're you talking about?' Alice asked.

Izzy looked towards Carol who gave her a slight nod of the head.

'Your mum's waiting to get results back.'

Alice looked panic stricken. 'For what?'

'An x-ray she had taken a few days ago,' Izzy said.

Kerry turned to look at Carol. This was the first she'd heard of it. Surely the agency would have informed her if it was true. She knew exactly what Izzy was up to and she wasn't going to be a party to it.

'But—'

Izzy stood and cut Kerry off before she could say anymore. 'Kerry, would you mind excusing us? As you can see, this is a private family matter.'

Kerry looked over at Alice who was sat in a daze.

'And don't worry about coming back tonight. Izzy's staying over so we've got everything covered,' Carol added with glee.

And that was it. She was fired without being fired. Without saying a word, Kerry gathered her belongings. At that moment, she didn't care that she was going to take a financial hit. All that was of concern to Kerry was Alice's wellbeing.

Her throat was dry, but she forced herself to speak normally. She wasn't going to give them the pleasure of knowing that they'd won. 'I understand.'

Once outside, she stopped to take stock of what had happened in the restaurant.

She couldn't believe the levels to which Carol and Izzy would sink, just to ensure Alice didn't escape their clutches.

While it was shocking, it didn't come as a surprise.

For the first time, Kerry understood why Alice's sister Emily had decided to go no contact with Carol.

Who would want to be part of a family when the family roots were rotten to the core?

Chapter Twenty-Eight

'Hello?' Emily called out as she pushed open her front door and released the key from the lock. 'Alice, are you here?'

No response.

Sure she was alone, Emily made her way to the kitchen. She searched frantically through the wall cabinets until she found what she was looking for. A bottle of whisky she always kept in the house for emergencies. Quickly unscrewing the cap on the bottle, she sniffed suspiciously at the contents and recoiled slightly at its pungent aroma. Spirits weren't her normal go to drink, but she needed something that would have a quick effect on her.

Something that would stop her hands from trembling.

She grabbed a mug from the sink, poured in a large measure and knocked it back in one go.

Once the coughing fit that ensued, caused by the onslaught of the fiery liquid, subsided, she poured another measure and knocked that one back too. The alcoholic burn disappeared within seconds and she welcomed the calming warmth that spread throughout her body. The calmness that now resided inside her was in stark contrast to how she'd felt while at Maggie's.

Her emotional response had caught her by surprise – it was such a shock to hear Maggie's side of things. Emily had been blindsided from start to finish. The question which begged an answer was whether or not she actually believed Maggie. From her point of view, Maggie had no reason to lie. Her dad was dead. There was nothing to gain. What was left of his will had been used to pay off the debt he had acquired.

Emily gazed out the window in deep thought. The web of lies that they had found themselves in had been spun by the people that were meant to care about them. Instead, they'd been pushed and pulled from pillar to post not knowing the truth.

Had their father abandoned them for another woman? A younger model. Someone who offered her dad freedom. Who kept his children from being able to see him? Or was it simply the case that their mother hated their father and wanted to destroy him. What better way to do that than separate him from the family he loved?

No, she couldn't believe that, because if she did, she would have to accept that it was she who had abandoned her father. She was the one who had ignored him and his late-night phone calls begging her to talk. It was Emily that was the callous one – who had hung up on him and switched off her phone only to change numbers the next day.

And what of those unopened letters? The ones in the loft gathering dust because she hadn't wanted to know what he had to say, but she couldn't find it in herself to throw them away. Just in case… a day like today happened.

She finished her mug of whisky and added another measure.

But what of her mother? Yes, Emily knew she was a devious, conniving woman who thought nothing of anyone but herself, but what had she got out of playing the victim? It wasn't as if anyone had paid her any attention. Or did she get enough attention simply by knowing that she was punishing their father by withholding his children from him?

If it turned out to be true, and Maggie was being honest, Emily didn't think she would be able to forgive herself. Not for everything she'd done. Not to mention the things she'd said.

Upstairs in the loft, Emily had no problem locating the letters. They were in the exact place she'd left them eight years ago. The last one arriving shortly before he died.

It was then she had hidden them. Shutting his memory out of her mind like a bad dream.

Settling down on the dusty floor next to the old wooden trunk, she lifted the lid and slid her hand in. Seconds later, she brought out a pile of letters. For their age they looked in surprisingly good condition.

She could already feel tears sting the back of her eyes as she smoothed her fingers across the envelopes, knowing that her father had once touched them.

Settling back against the trunk, she stretched her legs out in front of her and flicked through the dozens of letters he'd sent. In the end, she decided to go by the date stamp on the front of the envelope. It would be a time-consuming job, but it wasn't like she had anywhere to be. As she began to sort the letters out into separate piles, she made a promise to herself. No matter how painful the experience of reading her dad's words were going to be, she was going to push through it.

She had to get to the bottom of the secrets and lies. That was the only way she would be able to put an end to the generational curse of unhappiness bestowed on their family.

Chapter Twenty-Nine

Rain fell heavily from the grey leaden clouds, but Alice didn't care, didn't seem to notice as she walked slowly around the park looking at everything and nothing. People rushed by in desperate need of shelter from the downpour, and Alice couldn't help but wonder where they were all going to. Did they have a mother like hers? Someone they loved and hated at the same time? Or a sister that wasn't there for them in their time of need?

Alice knew there was no point in trying to reach out to Emily. She'd probably laugh at her and tell her what a fool she was – not that she blamed her.

Trying to see the best in people at all times was a trait of Alice's that caused major hinderances in her life and made her susceptible to staying in relationships a lot longer than she should have.

Best to follow my gut instinct from now on rather than what's deemed the 'right thing'.

It was a great surprise when Kerry came to her rescue. Interjecting in the conversation with a supportive comment was the last thing she expected. Especially knowing that it came with a hefty price to pay.

Alice knew her mother inside out and realised the moment Kerry defended her, she would no longer be welcome at her mother's house. Izzy had probably been fanning the flames, so Kerry didn't stand a chance. It was a good thing, Alice decided as she headed back to her car. It was one thing for her to be caught up in the toxic relationship with her mother and quite another for someone as nice and stable as Kerry. She remembered how she had spent her whole life walking on eggshells in order not to upset her mother and spark one of her tantrums. Or worse, the dreaded silent treatment which could stretch out for days and even months depending on the severity of the emotional injury Carol had imagined was caused.

Climbing into her car, Alice shrugged her wet jacket off and placed it in the passenger seat.

Now what? Where did she go from here? She didn't want to return to Emily's because Emily would instinctively pick up that something was wrong, and the last thing Alice needed was to see her gloating about being proven right. Visiting Stella wasn't an option, as she was still at her retreat, somewhere that sounded like absolute heaven right about now. To do nothing but meditate all-day would-be bliss.

Which left her with only one place to go. The only place she really wanted to be.

Alice pulled out her phone and tapped in a quick message. Seconds later she received a reply.

A smile curved her lips, an action that minutes ago would have seemed impossible.

Slipping her seatbelt across her chest and clicking it in, Alice turned on the engine and manoeuvred her car into the slow-moving traffic.

It took less than fifteen minutes for Alice to arrive at her destination. Then another two and she was knocking on the door. The footsteps seemed to rhyme with the beating of her heart.

When the door opened, and she saw Kerry's face, her heart went into overdrive.

No words were spoken. Just a sad smile, before Kerry stepped over the threshold and held Alice in her arms.

Without having to be told, Kerry knew. This alone brought tears to Alice's eyes as she let herself be comforted and gently rocked.

'Come on, let's get you inside,' Kerry said softly.

Taking hold of her hand, Kerry led her into the living room.

'Nice place,' Alice said taking in the inviting space.

'Thanks, excuse the mess.'

'Mess?' Alice laughed as she walked around the room inspecting the many photos on the wall. 'This place is immaculate.'

Kerry gestured for her to sit on the sofa and she reluctantly did so, wanting to carry on seeing if she could get a glimpse into Kerry's life through the photos. Especially the ones she assumed were of Kerry's deceased partner. Each of the many images portrayed a couple madly in love. Even from behind a lens, she could sense the bond they both shared. It deeply saddened her to think that Kerry had lost her soulmate.

'I'm so sorry about earlier.'

'You're sorry? About what?'

Kerry offered a regretful smile. 'That I didn't speak up. You know they were lying about the x-ray?'

Kerry's gaze traced Alice's face and when their eyes finally met, Alice saw they were full of compassion. She swallowed hard. Normally, Alice would have brushed it off and said the usual spiel about her mother not meaning to shame her in public, or that she was just having a bad day. Alice was too weary to lie anymore.

The person Kerry witnessed in the restaurant was the real Carol – day in day out. Had been since as far back as Alice could remember.

Yet for the first time, she didn't feel the need to lie, to cover for her. There was no doubt in her mind that Carol was at home now slagging her off to Izzy who she was sure would be agreeing with her.

In that moment, Alice realised she no longer cared About her mother's validation. She was never going to get it no matter what she did, so it was pointless trying anymore. She was done!

Alice dabbed at the single tear that slid down her cheek. 'I thought as much, but I don't need protecting, Kerry.'

'I know you don't, but you do need support and understanding.'

'I don't—'

Kerry stopped abruptly. 'Yes, you do, Alice. There's no shame in having needs.'

Alice knew she was retracting into defensive mode. A place where she pushed back and told the world she didn't need anyone's help. That she was fine on her own. But the simple truth was that she wasn't, and she did need support. She was just too scared to ask for it. Had been all her life. Her mother led her to believe that love and making a connection with someone showed a sign of weakness. So Alice had built a wall around herself and refused to let anyone in.

Oh how she could see it all so clearly now.

How she'd tried to remain small and unassuming, so her mother didn't feel threatened by her successes or small victories. When she was hired by the swanky city bank, she'd lied to her mother and told her the bank was relatively unknown. When Carol found out the truth, she hadn't spoken to Alice for two weeks, and even then, it was to tell her it would only be a matter of time before they realised she was incompetent and would fire her.

'I know,' Alice finally said.

The relief of someone else seeing the truth was like lifting a heavy load off her shoulders.

'D'you want to talk about it?'

Alice shook her head. One step at a time.

'Not now. Some other time perhaps.'

'I'll always be here. Even if it's over email.'

Alice winced. 'Oh about my travel plans. I should've told you.'

'No, you shouldn't have. It wouldn't have made any difference.'

'Are you sure?'

'Very. I wasn't expecting you to propose the next day and for the pair of us to ride off into the sunset together.'

Alice grinned. 'It's not a bad image.'

'No,' Kerry said returning her smile, 'but it's an unrealistic one.'

Alice was assailed with a daunting hollowness that centred in her chest. Alice thought their connection had been a strong one, Kerry clearly thought otherwise.

'Do you want something to drink?' Kerry said, breaking the awkward silence.

'No, I think I'd better go. I only came to say goodbye.' Alice stood.

'Oh, OK.' Kerry cast her eyes downward.

'Oh and I wanted to say sorry about you losing your job looking after my mum.'

Kerry looked up, measuring Alice with an uncertain look of appraisal. 'Can I be totally honest with you?'

'Of course.' Alice stared back waiting in silence. She knew what was coming.

'After seeing how your mum treated you today, I would've asked to be transferred to another patient anyway.'

Alice went to speak but Kerry quickly interrupted her, adding, 'I don't mean that in a judgemental way. I'm sure your mum has her reasons for the way she is, but I care about you, Alice. Rightly or wrongly, I wouldn't have been able to carry out my duties without wondering how she could be so hurtful to her own daughter.'

Alice took a step towards her. 'I appreciate what you're saying, but you shouldn't be out of a job because of me.'

'It's over. Let's forget about it.' Kerry's arms encircled Alice's waist. 'I'm going to miss you.'

'I'm gonna miss you too.'

Alice rested her forehead against Kerry's, staring at her intently.

Kerry's eyes were magnetic. Compelling. Evoking a need in Alice to connect with her. To feel wanted. A desire to lose herself in their lovemaking, even if it was for only one more time.

Kerry held out her hand and Alice took it, letting herself be led along the hallway and into a room Alice assumed was the guest bedroom, as it was devoid of any personal belongings.

'Are you sure you want to do this here?'

Alice's question was answered with a deep, long passionate kiss.

'I've got a secret to tell you,' Alice said as she lay down on the bed with Kerry.

Kerry unbuttoned Alice's shirt and pushed it back off her shoulders. 'Another one?'

Alice playfully bit Kerry's ear and whispered. 'I fancied you from the moment I laid eyes on you.'

Kerry blushed slightly, sucking in a deep breath as she unclipped Alice's bra and removed it. 'The feeling was totally mutual.'

Alice loved the fact that they could be open and honest with each other about their emotions. Being vulnerable and exposed had never felt safe with Izzy. Looking back now, she saw that there had been an invisible wall between them. What hurt the most was that Izzy never even tried to see behind Alice's veil. She had been happy enough for them to co-exist in a bubble of inauthenticity.

Up until now Alice hadn't known any different.

And she probably never would have had she not met Kerry.

Chapter Thirty

Kerry watched as Alice dressed in silence but the chatter in her mind was in overdrive. She had to tell her the truth. Not because she thought anything was going to come of it. The simple fact was that she didn't want to harbour any secrets. Alice deserved better than that. She would not be a clone of Alice's mother, and that meant no mind games. No push and pull with her emotions, and definitely no building up a wall of silence.

'Alice.'

'Mmm.' Alice turned to face her with a carefree grin as she buttoned her jeans and bent over to slip on her boots.

It made Kerry's heart leap to see her looking so happy. She hoped what she had to tell her wasn't going to change that.

'There's a chance I might be pregnant.'

It took a few moments for her words to sink in before Alice let out a small burst of laughter.

'I hope I'm not the daddy.' The laughter faded and confusion clouded her eyes when Kerry remained silent. 'Oh, so you're bi?'

'No.'

'No? Sorry if I'm being dim, Kerry, but you're not making any sense.'

'I might be having Sarah's baby.'

Alice blinked rapidly as the penny finally dropped.

With raised eyebrows, Alice gave her a questioning look. 'You used Sarah's eggs?'

Kerry nodded.

Alice averted her gaze, choosing to pay full attention to buttoning her shirt, as if it was the most pressing job that needed doing.

'Is that all you have to say?' Kerry asked in growing frustration. She'd expected something more than such a lacklustre response.

Alice inhaled a deep breath. 'When will you find out if it's worked?'

'Soon.'

Alice moved to the bed and sat down beside her. 'So that's why you took a second job at the agency?'

Kerry nodded again. 'I wanted to make sure I could afford to bring up a baby without relying on the state.'

Kerry would have loved to have been privy to Alice's mind as she couldn't tell what she was thinking from her expressionless face.

'A mini-Kerry, huh?' A small smile crept onto Alice's lips. 'I don't know what to say. Congratulations?'

'Thanks.'

Panic arose in Alice's eyes and she jerked back slightly. 'Hey, we couldn't have hurt—'

'No, sex is fine, Alice. Besides, you're gentle.'

They stared at each other across a sudden silence before Alice broke it in a tender voice.

'I'm happy for you, Kerry, I really am. I wish I was going to be around when you get the good news.'

'I can email you or do it the good old-fashioned way and just phone. I mean, that's if you want me to,' Kerry said nonchalantly, she had no intention of falling apart, at least not until she was alone.

'I'd like that more than anything,' Alice said with sincerity. 'I don't want to lose contact with you. No matter where I am in the world.'

'That means a lot to me.'

Alice reached out and gently stroked her stomach. 'They're going to be a lucky kid having a mummy like you.'

Kerry saw the sadness in her eyes, and not for the first time, wished she could rid Alice of the demons she knew dwelt within her.

'You'll meet them one day.'

'I hope so.'

Kerry bit her bottom lip to stem the cry that begged for release. In a matter of minutes, Alice was going to walk out of the door and out of her life.

There was no point in carrying on the conversation about her pregnancy. Kerry had no doubt that once Alice was thousands of miles away, she'd be the last thing on her mind. It hurt but it was reality.

'When do you leave?'

'Friday.'

'So soon?'

'There's nothing to make me stay.' Alice immediately clasped her hand over her mouth. 'I didn't mean—'

'It's OK, I know, and I'm glad you're getting away. If I was you, I would keep as much distance between you and your mum as you possibly can. You've got one life, Alice, and you need to live it on your terms without guilt, fear or obligation to anyone else.'

Alice took her hand and squeezed it. 'I wish I would've met you years ago.'

Kerry sighed. 'No, we met at the right time, which is now. Our paths crossed for a reason.'

'Only for us to part?'

'That's the beauty of life, we never know what's going to happen from one day to the next.'

Kerry's phone rang in the living room and she made to get out of bed. 'It might be work. I'd better get it.'

Alice followed her out of the bedroom.

'Hello… please listen… I can explain… Hello, hello…' Kerry looked down at the phone in disbelief.

'Who was that?'

'My boss from the agency. They've suspended me while they investigate a complaint your mum's made against me. Fuck!'

Kerry paced the floor. She knew Carol wouldn't stop there. Next, she'd probably call the hospital, that's if the agency didn't do it first. How had she let things come to this? She touched her stomach and guilt rose in her as she questioned whether or not she had done the right thing trying for a baby.

'Listen, don't stress yourself out, it won't do you any good.'

'And you think being unemployed will? Fuck! What a fucking mess.'

'I'll sort this, Kerry. I'll go and speak to my mum. I'll make her retract her complaint. I'll go and see your boss myself.'

'It'll only make things worse. Your mum's got it in for me now. I'm sure Izzy had a hand in this as well.'

Alice grabbed her jacket. 'They won't get away with this. I swear to God they won't.'

Alice stormed out of the room. Moments later the front door slammed. Then a car engine and screeching tyres sounded from outside.

Kerry didn't know what Alice intended to do but she couldn't just sit around and wait. She needed to do something, but what?

She quickly made a call. Hearing the distress in her voice, Debbie told her to sit tight.

It could have been minutes or hours before Debbie turned up, Kerry didn't know, as she sat in the same position feeling as if she was in a trance.

Her life's work was going up in smoke for one mistake. One that she knew she shouldn't have made, but there was no way she could turn back the clock and undo it now.

***

'I'm sorry I suggested you go to that agency,' Debbie said as she came through the front door half an hour later.

Debbie was just as furious as Alice had been. Kerry poured Debbie a large glass of wine to calm her down.

'No—'

Debbie held up her hand. 'If they can believe the lies from a woman who sounds like she has major issues, they don't deserve you.'

Kerry joined her at the dining table, enviously eyeing Debbie's wine, knowing that she didn't dare take a drop, just in case… 'But I was in the wrong, Debs.'

'No, you weren't. Alice isn't your client. What you do outside of work is no one's business.'

'Esther doesn't seem to think so.' Kerry swallowed hard, close to tears. It was bad enough losing her job – she could easily get another – but she couldn't restore her reputation if Esther got in touch with the hospital.

'You need to call her back?' Debbie said, as if she'd found the answer to world peace.

'And say what?'

'That you're goin' to mount an appeal.' Debbie took hold of Kerry's hands and looked pleadingly at her. 'Please, Kerry, do it now before this gets out of hand.'

Kerry picked up her mobile phone from the table and stared at it for a few seconds as she debated whether or not she would just be digging herself a bigger hole. Esther had sounded majorly pissed off when she'd called earlier.

Looking over at Debbie, Kerry realised she had no choice. Things would only escalate if she didn't face it head on.

Kerry called Esther back, clearing her voice when she answered.

'Esther—'

'Kerry, there's no point in us talking any further.' Esther got straight to the point. 'Yes, you're right, what you do in your private life is none of our concern but when you're having sex on duty—'

Kerry gasped and looked over at Debbie, unsure of what she'd just heard. 'Hold on a second… what did you say?'

'You were reported for having sex at the client's residence while she slept in the room next door. A time when an incident had taken place and the police were called—'

'She's lying and I can prove it. The police were there when Carol went off with Mary, her neighbour. I have the police statement which will prove she's lying. I'll be getting in touch with my union about this matter.'

She heard the doubt in Esther's voice. 'Bring me the statement first thing in the morning and let's sort this mess out.'

Kerry looked towards Debbie and said a silent thank you to her.

Chapter Thirty-One

Her mother had gone too far this time. It was one thing for Alice to be on the receiving end of her malice, but quite another for it to be aimed at someone who was completely innocent and had done nothing but be supportive of her.

Alice arrived at Emily's, no longer afraid to admit that she had been wrong all these years. She'd lived in self-denial about who her mother was as a person. Emily had tried to extract her from their mother's toxic web, but Alice had believed her mother's lies over her sister's truth.

No more.

Alice's eyes were wide open now, and before she left to pursue her dream around the world, she had several wrongs to right.

'Emily!' Alice called as she entered the hallway. Such was her urgency, she didn't bother closing the door.

Not hearing a response, Alice checked Emily's office. Empty. She moved on to the rest of the rooms on the ground floor. All of which were empty. As she reached the bottom of the stairs Emily came into view. Even from a distance, Alice could tell she'd been crying. Alice slowly mounted the stairs, tentatively taking one step at a time.

'What's wrong, Lee?' Alice asked, fearful of hearing

the reply. Emily didn't cry unless it was something bad. Hell, she hadn't even cried when their father died.

'We need to talk.'

'I know, and I need to apologise.'

Emily looked at her questioningly as she neared. 'For what?'

'Everything. You were so right about Mum. Probably Dad too.'

Emily shook her head. 'No, I wasn't. I've never been so wrong in my life,' Emily said, lowering herself onto the top step.

Alice almost did a double take as she tried to figure out what Emily meant. Was she now saying her opinion of their parents was flawed? Alice was starting to feel as if she was in a parallel universe where everything was topsy turvy. For years, Emily had insisted their parents were just short of being the devil themselves and now, here she was telling Alice she'd made a mistake.

Alice waited patiently for Emily to begin speaking and when she remained silent, Alice's gaze was inadvertently drawn to a piece of paper Emily clutched in her hand.

Resisting the urge to take it from her, Alice gently touched her leg to bring her back to the moment and make her realise she was waiting for a response.

'I went to see Maggie,' Emily finally said.

Alice froze. Whatever words she would normally have responded with were now stuck in her throat, lodged there like a blockage.

'I had to,' Emily said, looking Alice straight in her

eyes. 'Arnold told me—'

'Hold on a minute,' Alice said, swallowing past the lump in her throat. 'You've seen Arnold too? What's going on, Lee. Have you had a reunion with Dad's friends?'

'If I didn't, he was going to dispute my version of events.'

'So what? We know what the truth is.'

'That's just it, we don't. We've been lied to all our lives.'

'Lied to? About what?'

'Everything.'

Alice was on her feet in seconds. 'Will you get to the point and stop fucking going 'round in circles. I don't think I can take much more today.'

'Maggie wasn't dad's partner.'

Alice let her words sink in. 'But he lived with her for over fifteen years.'

'I know but only as a friend. He rented one of her rooms from her.'

'So what're you saying then?' The penny dropped. Her stomach clenched so tightly it hurt. That was the big secret. The thing that had torn her family apart from the start. 'Are you saying that Arnold and Dad…'

Emily looked mollified as she shook her head. 'No, Alice, Dad and Arnold weren't lovers.'

Alice slumped back down on the stair again and held her face in her hands. 'I don't understand. Why would Dad lead us to believe that Maggie was his partner if she wasn't?'

This was a total head fuck and, in that moment, Alice wanted to return to her room, pack her case and get the first flight out of London. She'd had enough.

Emily shrugged. 'Do you actually remember Dad introducing her to us as anything but a friend?'

'No…' The cogs in Alice's brain began to turn. Slowly at first, then they began to build momentum. 'Mum… was the… one that told us.'

'Exactly, along with everything else we know about Dad.'

'But why would she lie about something like that?' Alice asked before realising she knew why. The woman was evil. In the past and the present.

'Because that's just the person that she is. And do you want to know the worst thing about all this?'

Alice shook her head not trusting herself to speak.

'Dad still loved her until the end.' Tears welled in Emily's eyes. 'Maggie said he was looking for her on his death bed, hoping he'd see her one last time.'

The thought of her dad still pining for their mother now brought tears to Alice's eyes too. Did her mother feel the same way about him? In all the years since their dad left, Carol had not so much as looked at another man. Not that she hadn't had the opportunity.

'So why did he leave her? Us?'

'Are you sure you want to know?'

Alice nodded, though deep down she wasn't a hundred percent sure she really did want to. 'Yes, nothing can be as bad as I'm imagining.'

Emily dropped a bombshell that literally shook her

world and tore it to pieces.

'Dad was infertile.'

Emily looked at Alice obviously waiting for a reaction. Getting none, she spoke again.

'Did you hear what I said? Dad was infertile.'

It wasn't that Alice hadn't heard her. She had. Loud and clear. It was simply that Alice didn't know what to say. She couldn't find the right words to relay how she felt. The implications of what Emily had said were too unbearable to contemplate.

If her dad was infertile that meant…. That meant… she couldn't bring herself to think of what it meant, how the consequences of knowing would change her life forever. It was only her mind that would acknowledge Emily's words, her hurt was too fragile for such a blow.

It would shatter into a thousand pieces if what Emily was saying was true.

Alice looked down at the letter in Emily's hand again, more to buy time than anything else.

'What's that?'

Emily gazed into the distance, taking a few moments before speaking again. 'One of the many letters Dad sent me over the years.'

'He sent you letters…?' The shock on Alice's face must have spoken volumes because Emily finished her unfinished sentence, words that Alice wouldn't speak out loud.

'Despite the shitty way I treated him.'

'I didn't mean—'

'I know you didn't but it's the truth. All these years

we've blamed him for leaving us when it was all down to her.'

'Can I see it?' Alice said, referring to the letter.

'Sure,' Emily handed it to her.

Alice took the letter from her hand and pressed it against her chest, feeling a stab of sadness, she unfolded the letter and read it. Slowly, the words on the page swam from side to side, up and down. As she read each line, her heart broke all over again. She could sense the anguish from his written words.

Tears fell on the page smudging blue ink. Then without warning, Emily, her sister, her once confidante, moved down a step and gathered her in her arms where they wept together like helpless children.

'We'll get through this,' Emily reassured Alice through her own sobs.

Emily was back.

'What are we going to do?'

'Do we have to do anything?'

'Of course. We can't let her think she's got away with this. Especially after the stunt she pulled today.'

Emily raised her eyebrows, a questioning look in her eyes.

'Mum's nurse…' Alice paused not sure how to explain the situation without making both herself and Kerry look bad.

'Go on,' Emily pressed. 'Nothing that woman does could shock me.'

'It's just a bit awkward.'

'You slept with the nurse?' Emily said matter-of-factly. There was no judgement in her voice nor her expression.

Alice gave a relieved smile that she didn't have to spell it out. 'Yeah.'

'I take it you broke up with Izzy first?' Emily said, her forehead creasing in confusion.

'I did. She cheated on me.'

'Aww, so that's why you ended up here?'

Alice exhaled a breath and nodded, ashamed of herself. She had let their mother build a wall between them when she should have known better. But Alice had wanted their mother's love so badly, she had been willing to throw Emily under the bus to obtain it.

'Would you have got in touch if you didn't need somewhere to stay?'

'Eventually,' Alice answered honestly. 'I hated not being able to see you. Especially as it's my own fault for just cutting you off without talking things through.'

'What's done is done, I suppose.'

Alice looked down at her hands. 'I've missed you.'

'I've missed you too,' Emily said softly.

Alice's voice rose an octave. 'I can't believe that woman has got away with manipulating us for so long. Well not you, me.'

'What did she do? You mentioned the nurse?'

'To cut a long story short, we had lunch together and Mum started her normal nonsense so Kerry stood up for me.'

Emily pulled a face. 'Ouch.'

'Yep, but d'you know what? It took something as

minute as that for the fog to lift from my eyes.'

'You were in too deep to see. It wasn't that you didn't know, you just didn't want to. I fought it myself, but I had to get out. She was suffocating me. I knew you wouldn't listen to me, but I always hoped one day you'd meet someone who showed you her behaviour isn't normal.'

It was strange but true. Carol would still get away with her behaviour if Kerry hadn't entered Alice's life and made her face reality.

'She overstepped the mark by getting Kerry caught up in this mess. She called Kerry's workplace and told them we'd slept together, and now she's under investigation.'

'What! That…' Emily stood up, holding her hand out to her. 'Come on.'

'Where're we going?' Alice asked as she took Emily's extended hand.

'To finally make that woman accountable for all the trouble she's caused.'

Alice didn't need telling twice. She slid her hand into Emily's, and they made their way down the stairs side by side. Reunited at last.

Apart they were weak.

Together they were invincible.

Chapter Thirty-Two

The look on Carol's face when she opened the door told Alice this was the last thing she'd expected. Both daughters on her doorstep. Together. For a split second, Carol looked hesitant, as if she was considering slamming the door shut but thought better of it. As always, her mother would fight her own corner whether she was in the right or wrong.

'We need to talk,' Emily said.

'There's nothing I want to hear from either of you. As far as I'm concerned, you're both dead to me.'

'Jesus, when are you gonna stop?!'

Carol blinked rapidly, taken aback. 'Excuse me?'

'The lies. Hurting people, you've got to stop.'

It was rare to see Emily react to their mother. In fact, it was rare for Emily to lose her temper, let alone raise her voice, but Alice knew on this occasion it had more to do with the gradual build-up of the injustice of their mother's actions than anything else. Even Alice herself could feel her blood boiling just being in Carol's presence.

'I don't know what you're talking about.' The panic in Carol's voice was clear to hear and Alice couldn't help but wonder how many secrets she had in her closet. It was obvious she didn't know which one Emily could possibly be referring to which made Alice think there must be a lot.

Alice didn't know why, considering how many times they'd played this game, but she still couldn't believe the bare-faced cheek of her mother, standing there in front of them looking like butter wouldn't melt in her mouth, when both daughters knew exactly what level she'd stoop to in order to get her own back.

'I know why Dad left and the lies you told us.' Emily spat the words at her in disgust.

'What lies? He ran off with that whore.'

'Except he didn't, did he? You kicked him out after cheating on him.'

Carol smirked. 'Who told you that rubbish?'

Alice leant forward, the bitterness in her voice evident. 'Maggie herself.'

Carol clapped her hand to her chest. 'And you believe her over me? Your own mother?'

'You just can't stop the lies, can you? Are you going to tell us who our real father is?' Alice asked.

Carol pushed the door forward instinctively. In that moment, Alice saw in her eyes that what Maggie had said was true. If she hadn't wanted to believe it before, she had no choice now.

Alice jammed her foot in the doorway, suppressing the urge to scream as the door made contact with her foot.

Silence.

'Look, whatever Arnold told you, it's all lies. He isn't your father.'

Alice's throat constricted as she and Emily turned to each other at the same time, their expressions matching one another's. Mouths slightly agape, they gave a slight shake of their heads. Alice knew Emily was having the same thoughts as herself. Why had Carol automatically jumped to the conclusion that Arnold had anything to do with Emily's comment.

Erratic thoughts raced through Alice's mind as she tried to connect the dots, but she couldn't. None of it made any sense.

Puzzled, shaken, Alice fought the natural desire to retreat and run. Far away so she didn't have to think that her whole life had been a lie and the perpetrator had been her own mother.

Out of nowhere, she heard Emily's voice, measured and calm. 'There's nothing we can do about our past now, but we can stop you from ruining someone else's life. You need to contact the nursing agency and tell them you made a mistake.'

Carol's chest puffed out as if she was ready for battle. 'I'll do no such thing.'

'In which case you leave me no other choice than to expose you and the wicked things you did to our father.'

'And how would you do that exactly?'

'You're going to find out sooner or later, so I might as well tell you now, I'm writing dad's biography.'

Carol looked perplexed for a moment before the severity of Emily's threat seemed to sink in.

'You're doing what?'

Emily took a step forward.

'You heard me.'

Carol's face paled. 'But you can't.'

'Why can't I? I have Dad's letters. All of them, in his own handwriting. I'll happily hand them over to the media now as a way to drum up interest before my book's release. Just imagine what all your friends will think of you for having lied to them all these years about being the poor abandoned wife.'

The sound of Alice's heartbeat drowned out Carol's reply. All she could think of was how her father had been deemed a rotten scoundrel and he'd done absolutely nothing wrong. Their mother had ruined his good name to cover up her own affair.

She wanted it to be a lie. Needed it to be so she was to have even the slightest feeling of love for her mother, a love that had pretty much dwindled over the years.

'Well, what's it going to be? Emily said.

'Fine,' Carol finally said begrudgingly.

Emily took a step forward towards Carol. 'I want you to make the call in front of us.'

'Are you saying you don't trust me?' Carol asked, backing away.

Emily's expression said it all. She wouldn't trust her as far as she could throw her.

They waited in silence as Carol turned and walked unsteadily down the hallway. A few seconds later, muffled voices could be heard. Izzy was obviously inside. Alice was sure she had been the one who instigated the plan and her mother just ran with it to the finish line.

'I just don't understand why she behaves like this,'

Alice said on the verge of tears. 'Our own mother.'

'That's just it, Alice, it doesn't matter. She is the way she is and no matter how much you try to find a reason, you never will. She's not going to change. Just accept it the way I have.'

Alice's heart hurt at the complexities of her relationship with her mother. A part of her still wanted to believe that somewhere inside of Carol, she did love them. Cared for them as a mother should. But how could she when the evidence was the total opposite.

After a few minutes, Carol returned, phone in hand.

'I don't see why I'm being treated as the villain in all of this. I'm not the one—'

Emily rolled her eyes. 'Please just give it a rest will you and think of the damage you've already done.'

Carol glared at Emily before jabbing the digits on her phone. A snarl curled her lips which softened when her call was answered on the other end.

'Mrs Bridges here. Yes, I'm calling about an incident I reported earlier. Seems I was mistaken. Must have been the medication I took the night before messing with my head. Yes, I'd like to retract it.'

All sweetness and light. Alice wondered why her mother hadn't been an actress herself. She could switch personalities in a split second.

Saying goodbye, Carol snapped the phone shut.

'Look at the pair of you. You should be ashamed of yourselves, picking on a woman my age. And you…'

She stabbed a finger towards Emily. 'Your own

mother has a stroke and nearly dies, and you don't even ask how I am.'

Emily stifled a laugh. 'Nearly died? I bet you were back on the fags and booze the same day.'

There was a flicker of guilt in Carol's eyes which was soon replaced with contempt. 'You'd know what it's like to sacrifice your life for your children if you'd had the guts to have one.'

'That will never happen,' Emily said. 'This ends here with you. I wouldn't bring a child into this world even if there was a one percent chance of them carrying your genes.'

'There's nothing wrong with my genes. But there is something wrong with the pair of you. My own mother told me so.'

Alice shook her head. The heat rose fast and furiously to her cheeks.

'Mum! Really?' Alice raised her voice, angry and defensive. 'The hell you've put us through all of our lives, are you really going to blame us for your fuck ups too?'

Alice didn't care if her language was offensive to her mother anymore. She pretty much didn't care about her full stop. 'You lied to us about why dad left. It's because you kicked him out and were sleeping with his best friend.'

The fact that Carol couldn't meet her eyes and didn't deny Alice's accusation confirmed what she thought. *Mum and Arnold.* Just the image in her mind's eye grossed her out.

'I think that's enough now,' Izzy said authoritatively, coming up behind Carol. 'Do you want her to have another stroke?'

Emily ignored Izzy, looking straight into Carol's eyes. 'You know what the saddest thing is? Dad loved you until the end… despite everything.'

Alice thought she saw a glimmer of pain in her mother's eyes, but she couldn't be sure. Before anyone could say another word, Izzy pulled Carol back into the passage and slammed the door shut.

Emily took hold of Alice's arm and led her back to the car in silence. Once inside, the topic that neither of them wanted to talk about needed to be addressed.

'Do you think it's true then? That Arnold's our father?'

'Our biological father you mean,' Emily corrected her. 'Probably.'

'You don't seem that shocked.'

Emily sighed. 'That's because I'm not. That woman has done so many things, I wouldn't believe her if she told me the sky was blue. Besides, I always had an inkling there was a reason why Arnold seemed to take such an interest in us.'

Alice nodded slowly, remembering the many occasions Arnold would arrive and turn their birthdays or Christmas into a massive fanfare. Going completely overboard to spoil them. Then there'd be the arguments between her parents after he left. Their dad would get drunk and the shouting would continue for hours. In the morning, their mother would appear at breakfast with red swollen eyes pretending as if nothing had happened. Even then, she'd been playing the victim and Alice was too blind to see it.

'What are we going to do?'

Emily squeezed her hand. 'Nothing we can do. Just carry on as normal.'

'And what about your book? Are you going to tell the truth?'

'Yes, I'm going to re-write it and add his good side instead of just concentrating on his flaws.'

'I'm glad.'

'So d'you fancy going for a drink?'

'I'd love to, but I need to go somewhere first.'

Chapter Thirty-Three

Kerry opened her front door and blinked rapidly. Although she'd known Alice had a twin sister, she wouldn't have been able to tell the difference if it wasn't for the mole on her sister's face.

'Sorry to drop in unannounced but I wanted to let you know in person that my mum has retracted her statement.'

'I know. Esther just called to tell me. I don't know how you managed to change her mind but thank you.'

'There's nothing to thank me for. Emily's the one who had her on the ropes.'

Kerry noticed the pride in Alice's voice and couldn't help but smile. It was obvious they'd made up and she was more than happy for them. She couldn't help but wonder if fate had intervened just to bring the sisters back together again.

'Well thank you, Emily,' Kerry said, extending her hand for Emily to shake.

Emily smiled. 'It was a pleasure.'

'Please, come in.'

Kerry stepped back and indicated for them to enter. Once in the living room, she introduced the women to Debbie.

'Can I get you both something to drink?'

Alice shook her head, but Emily nodded. 'Tea would be great, thanks.'

'I'll make it,' Debbie said.

'So have you made up with your mum?'

'No,' Alice said with sadness in her voice. 'I think I've finally accepted that we're never going to have the kind of mother-daughter relationship I've always wanted. It'll be a case of having to love her from a distance.'

The word 'distance' triggered an overwhelming sadness within Kerry. She hadn't lost sight of the fact that Alice would no longer be a part of her life soon. That they would be saying their own goodbyes and moving on with their respective lives. A lump caught in her throat at the thought of never seeing Alice again.

How long would it take to forget her? Or would she even be able to?

It was like grieving all over again.

Did she regret it?

No. That was the risk you took when you opened your heart and were vulnerable.

Kerry thought of all the happy years she'd spent with Sarah, and despite the tragic ending, knew she wouldn't swap a second of it, even if she'd known beforehand what their future held.

Love was love, and anyone fortunate enough to find it twice in a lifetime was an incredibly lucky person.

Twice? Kerry hadn't realised that her heart had revealed its true feelings for the woman sat opposite her. The woman whose eyes reflected the same sadness she felt. Could it be that the feeling was mutual? The thought terrified yet excited her at the same time.

Debbie brought a tray of teas in and sat beside her.

'I wasn't being nosy, but I couldn't help overhearing your problem at the agency has been sorted?'

Kerry gave Emily a grateful look. 'Thanks to Emily.'

'I think we should have something a bit stronger than this to celebrate,' Emily said. 'What does everyone think?'

'Count me in,' Debbie said.

'Me too,' Alice said, staring expectantly at Kerry.

'I'd love to join you, but I can't drink.'

'You're not working tonight, are you?' Debbie asked.

'No, it's just that I might be pregnant. I don't know for sure, but everything has started to taste funny. Food, water and I've got a strange craving for gherkins and I hate gherkins. My mum said that's what happened to her when she was pregnant with me.'

It took a few seconds for the gravity of her statement to sink in. Debbie was first on her feet, bending over to embrace her.

'That's amazing, Kerry, oh my God, I'm gonna be an aunt.'

Kerry laughed and looked over at Alice whose expression was neutral, then at Emily who looked bemused.

'You might be pregnant?' Emily said, a puzzled expression on her face.

Kerry nodded. This wasn't the way she wanted to reveal the news to Alice, but she didn't want to be that person keeping secrets in her life. Alice had enough of that already.

'Congratulations,' Emily said, glancing over at Alice.

'Yeah, I'm happy for you,' Alice said. 'I really am.'

'Thanks, Alice, that means a lot to me.'

'Instead of booze, why don't we hit the ice cream parlour instead? A healthy dose of a Nutella crepe will go down a treat,' Debbie said.

'I can't. I just realised I still have a load of stuff to sort out before my flight on Friday.' Alice stood and Emily followed suit.

'It was nice meeting you both,' Emily said, then looked down at the untouched cups of tea. 'Sorry we don't have time to drink it.'

'Don't worry about it,' Kerry and Debbie said in unison.

'Right, I think I'll go and wait in the car,' Emily said, giving Alice's shoulder a reassuring squeeze.

'And I'll come with you. I heard you're a writer,' Debbie said. 'I'd love to pick your brains about a story idea.'

'Sure.'

Their voices trailed off until the front door slammed. Once they were alone, it was Alice who spoke first.

'You're going to be an amazing mum, Kerry,' Alice's voice choked with emotion.

'Thank you,' Kerry said fighting back the tears. 'And you're going to have a great time travelling the world and putting all this stuff with your mum behind you.'

'If only it was that simple.' Alice forced a laugh. 'But I'll try.'

'I'm going to miss you, Alice.' Kerry could no longer hold back the tears that welled in her eyes and let them graciously fall down her cheeks.

Alice stepped closer to her. 'I'm going to miss you too.'

Alice pressed her hand gently against Kerry's stomach. 'I want to hear all about this little guy growing inside of you. And when they arrive, I want lots of pictures.'

Kerry laughed through her sobs. 'And I want to see the world through your eyes.'

They instinctively reached out to each other and fell into a tight embrace.

'I wish things could've been different,' Alice said, her voice muffled from her mouth pressing against Kerry's shoulder.

'I'm only glad I met you.'

Although her heart was broken, Kerry wouldn't have turned back the clock even if she could. Yes, she wanted Alice to stay. To be in her life and help raise the baby that might be growing inside of her.

She would have liked to have helped banish the memory of Alice's mother's toxicity by raising a child together who they would love and support no matter what.

It was naïve to think that way she knew.

Kerry had seen the pity in Emily's eyes when she

had congratulated her on her pregnancy. It brought to light that both women were so emotionally scarred by their upbringing that they both feared for any child brought into the world. Carol had done such a number on them that they equated love with pain.

Kerry and Alice stood staring at one another, realising that it didn't matter what either of them genuinely wanted, it wasn't plausible.

Kerry wanted to be a mother more than anything in the world.

And Alice wanted her freedom.

Chapter Thirty-Four

What did I think was going to happen? That I could get emotionally attached to Kerry and just walk away as if she meant nothing to me. The same question had been going around and around on a loop in Alice's mind for the past few hours.

And now Kerry was pregnant which only served to complicate matters even further.

A flood of emotions had assaulted her at once – fear, anger, jealousy, repulsion, sorrow, pity. All vying for top spot, and in the end, sorrow won out.

Alice desperately wanted to feel happy for her, and deep down she did because of how much this pregnancy meant to her. Yet despite this, Alice could never be a part of her life now. Even if she wanted to. How could Alice be certain she wouldn't behave like her mother and start the cycle all over again. How could she trust herself around an innocent child, not to mess its head up and have yet another damaged member of the population. Where would it all end?

No, the decision she'd made not to get involved with Kerry was the right one. She knew that deep down in her heart.

'So as soon as my book's finished, I'll meet you in Mexico?' Emily's voice broke into Alice's thoughts. 'I've always wanted to go there.'

'Me too, it's going to be amazing sharing the

experience with you.'

'I wouldn't miss it for the world. It'll give us time to catch up as well.' Emily checked her watch. 'You've got ten minutes before we have to leave.

Alice zipped her case closed. 'I'm all done.'

'Can I ask you something?'

'Sure,' Alice said, placing her case on the floor and pulling the handle to its full length.

Emily eyed her warily, as if she couldn't make up her mind whether to speak her thoughts aloud.

After a few seconds, Emily exhaled a sigh and said, 'You don't think you're making a mistake, do you?'

Alice frowned. 'About travelling?'

'No, about leaving Kerry.'

Alice stared at her, not quite sure what to make of her comment. She wasn't leaving Kerry. To imply that, would mean that they had some sort of relationship or future together. They had neither. Kerry was going to have a baby, a decision she had obviously made a long time ago, way before she met Alice.

'I'm not leaving Kerry. She has her life to lead and I have mine.'

Emily remained silent but Alice knew something was up. That she had something she wanted to tell her but was trying to think of the right approach.

'Come on, out with it.'

Emily feigned innocence. 'What?'

'What's on your mind?'

Emily smiled, shaking her head. 'I can't believe I'm actually going to say this, but I think you're making a big mistake.'

'But I've always wanted to travel—'

'No, Alice, what you've always done is run away.'

Alice tried to make sense of her observation. Was there any truth in it? Had the cause of all of her break-ups been down to her in some way. Was she the common denominator? No, she told herself. Izzy cheated on her and that was something she was not going to take the blame for. As for the other women she'd dated, their relationships had ended due to them coming to a natural end.

'That is so not true, I—'

'Isn't it? How come all of your relationships end after two years?'

'Oh please, don't do a mother on me and make this about me. Izzy cheated on me.'

'But you moved on pretty quick by the sound of it.'

'Only because...' Alice paused, unable to finish the sentence. She knew if she did, she'd have to face the truth that she hadn't been in love with Izzy. She'd never been in love with anyone... Because the simple truth was that she didn't know how to love.

Alice slumped on the bed, feeling as if she'd been struck in the stomach.

She thought back to the internet searches she'd made over the years – how do you know if you love someone? How do you show someone you love them?

Shouldn't it have been instinctive? Second nature. Pretty much how she felt... about Kerry.

It was an undeniably strong connection – two

meetings of their souls. All of those before were of no comparison.

Emily sat beside her and draped her arm over her shoulders.

'Listen, with my crappy track record I'm the last person you should be listening to but Kerry, I think she would make you happy and vice versa.'

'She can't, you know I don't want kids. It wouldn't be fair on her.'

'But don't you see, you can face your past and get rid of mum's toxic influence by changing the life of someone else. You know I feel the same way about kids. And by that, I mean a biological child, but if I met a man who I fell in love with and he already had one, I'd be by him in a shot.'

'Really?' Alice wasn't totally convinced.

Emily laughed. 'OK, it might take time to warm to the idea, but what I'm trying to say is, if the kid is someone else's there's less chance of us screwing up. You can recognise the triggers before they can get a grip.'

'It wouldn't work, and I'd never forgive myself for giving Kerry false hope. She deserves someone who can make her happy and wants the same things she does. Plus, I really don't think she'd appreciate me using her baby as an "experiment" to heal my inner wounds.'

'You know it wouldn't be an experiment, Alice. You'd love that child as if it were your own. Don't let Mum take this from you. Don't you think she's taken enough?'

Alice's phone rang before she could respond.

Checking the ID, she saw Kerry's name on the screen.

'If this isn't fate, I don't know what is,' Emily said, grinning. 'Aren't you going to answer it?'

Alice rejected the call. She couldn't bear to hear Kerry's voice again. She had to be strong and let the cord that bound them break. 'No. We've said our goodbyes. There's no point in prolonging the agony.'

Alice got to her feet, took hold of her case, and moved towards the door. 'And you're wrong about mum. She hasn't taken anything from me. If it wasn't for her, I doubt I'd know what I wanted out of life.'

'If you say so, but I still think you're making a mistake.'

'If I am, I'll live with it, but at least the only person who'll suffer is me.'

The decision now firmly made in her mind, Alice gathered the rest of her belongings and made her way out to Emily's car.

Alice's phone broke the silence. An unknown number flashed up on the screen.

Her finger hovered over the reject button. It was probably her mother using someone else's number. Alice rejected the call. Seconds later it rang again.

Emily glanced over at her.

'Whoever that is, they're persistent. Don't you think you should answer it? It could be an emergency.'

'If it is and it's about Mum, I'd rather not know. Let Izzy look after her.'

'OK.'

They drove the rest of the journey to the airport in

silence. It took a hard effort not to think about why Kerry would have called her. There could have been a million and one reasons so there was no point in trying to guess.

'Do you want me to come inside?' Emily asked, pulling up outside the airport terminal.

'No, I'll only cry when you leave,' Alice said, feeling the ache start in her throat as she unbuckled her seat belt. She didn't want to leave Emily, and deep down she didn't want to leave Kerry either, but her head was in such a mess she needed to put some distance between everyone. Only then did Alice think she'd be able to finally find her true path.

'I'll be seeing you in a couple of months. Make sure you have a tequila sunrise waiting for me when I arrive.'

'I will,' Alice said, pulling Emily in for a hug. Her voice was full of emotion when she spoke. 'Take care, Lee.'

'You too,' Emily said, her own voice choked full of tears.

Alice climbed out of the car, retrieved her bag and case from the boot and quickly made her way into the airport, wiping the fallen tears from her cheeks. As she looked around for her check in area her phone rang again. The same unknown number.

She decided to answer this time. It didn't matter what ruse her mother used, she was at the airport now and there was no turning back. In a matter of minutes, she'd have checked in her case and been on her way through security.

She pressed accept and was confused for a few seconds by the voice at the other end, that was until Debbie said her name.

Almost immediately the blood in her veins ran cold. Debbie was crying. Hard.

'What's happened?' Alice almost screamed down the phone as she barged past on-comers as she ran to the exit. The connection dipped, only letting her hear dribs and drabs of the conversation.

'It's Kerry, she's lost… blood…'

'What hospital is she in?' Alice ran out of the airport, straight towards the taxi rank and knocked on the first cab she saw with its yellow light on.

The cab driver lowered his window, and she poked her head through. 'I need to get to St Thomas' hospital. It's an emergency.'

Without saying a word, the cab driver started the meter as soon as she jumped in the back and put her seat belt on.

Why the hell hadn't she answered the phone when Kerry called her? Why hadn't she been there for her? She imagined the fear Kerry must have felt being alone, not knowing whether the new life growing inside of her would survive.

She tried to gather her thoughts. There was no point in being hysterical until she knew what was going on. And even then, she had to remain calm – whatever the outcome.

She silently prayed it would be a happy one.

Despite the heavy traffic, the cab arrived in record

time and Alice tipped him generously for his effort. Debbie was waiting outside the reception for her.

'How is she?' Alice asked as they hurried through the corridor with great urgency.

'Scared.'

'I'm sorry I called you. Kerry told me not to as you're flying out today, but I didn't know what else to do. I tried ringing you from her phone but when you didn't pick up, I assumed you'd already left.'

'You did the right thing calling me,' Alice said glancing at her briefly. 'I'm glad you did.'

They arrived at the ward and a nurse who seemed to recognise Debbie let them in. Debbie led Alice straight to an almost bare side room on the ward where Kerry lay on a narrow metallic bed curled up in a foetal position.

Kerry looked so small and vulnerable that tears immediately sprung to Alice's eyes.

She roughly wiped them away, reminding herself she had to be strong. It's only when Alice switched off her mobile phone and put it in her bag that she remembered she was meant to be in the departure lounge at that moment in time. But Alice didn't care. There was no place she'd rather be than at Kerry's side.

The door opened and a nurse walked in, heading straight to Kerry to take her blood pressure. Kerry's eyes opened into slits before widening upon seeing Alice.

'Alice,' Kerry groaned, like she was just coming around after being knocked out on heavy medication.

Alice stood and went to her, gently stroking her leg on top of the rough blue blanket.

'How're you feeling?'

'Sick, tired.'

'That's because you won't eat. You must get something down you,' the nurse said brightly.

The door opened again and this time a doctor walked in, a solemn look on her face. She looked from Alice to Kerry, waiting for the nurse to retreat from the room before she walked over to the bedside.

'I've just received your results.' The doctor left the words hanging in the air as she flicked through the papers in the folder she held in her hands.

Alice took a deep breath in anticipation and held it until she could feel herself go dizzy. If she was going to faint, at least she was in the right place.

Chapter Thirty-Five

Emily stood there for a moment, staring at the front door, doubt flooding her mind. Was she opening Pandora's box when it should be left firmly closed? Probably, but she had to do it. Had to find out the truth. And who better to hear it from but the man himself – Arnold.

When he opened the door a few minutes later, he looked genuinely surprised to see her. And pleased. He stepped back to let her in, and she walked straight in the direction of the living room.

Arnold followed slowly behind her.

'Can I get you something to drink?' Arnold said as he entered the room.

There was a fiery determination in her voice when she spoke. She was done with all the lies and secrets. If Arnold was their father, she wanted to know once and for all. The fallout she would deal with later. 'I'm not here for pleasantries, Arnold, I'm here—'

'I know why you're here.'

He lowered himself onto his seat with great difficulty and looked at her sideways. Pain etched on his features.

'Then that saves me the humiliation of having to ask.'

'You've got to understand, Lee, Clyde was a hard man to deal with.'

'What's this got to do with anything?'

'It has everything to do with it. The reason I sent you over to Maggie's was so you could get a feel on the type of person he was. He trusted no one.'

'With good reason,' Emily interjected.

'Please hear me out before you start jumping to conclusions.'

Emily held herself in check as she stared at the man who could potentially be her father. If it turned out it was him, where did they go from here? She couldn't simply wipe the memories of Clyde from her mind and automatically look at Arnold as her father. Not that she would even want to. Her dad had been deceived by the two people he should have been able to trust with his life. None of what happened was his fault, and that's what she intended to tell Arnold if he kept trying to come up with excuses for this behaviour.

Emily sat opposite him and nodded for him to carry on.

'As you know, me and your mum were close. I'd met her before she met Clyde and fell madly in love with him. He was someone I could never compete with. He had everything Carol wanted apart from being able to give her kids.'

Her breath was shallow and hard. *Oh fuck, it is true, Arnold's our dad.*

Emily was on her feet again, now pacing the room with listless energy.

'Do you want to hear this?' Arnold asked.

'I don't have much choice now, do I?' Emily

snapped at him and immediately felt ashamed of herself. He was a fragile old man and she needed to bear that in mind instead of lashing out. 'I'm sorry, carry on.'

'The doctors told him when he went in for an operation on his private parts. Your mum said she didn't care but as the years went on things became contentious between them.'

And you shagged her and got her pregnant. Charming!

'Then one day Clyde turns up at my place, so legless he could barely stand. He told me Carol was pregnant. Of course, I was happy for him. I thought they'd finally be able to sort out their differences and have the family they'd always wanted.'

Emily raised her eyebrows. This sudden turn in the story wasn't what she'd been expecting to hear. Was he indirectly telling her that he hadn't had an affair with Carol? That there had been other men and her biological father could be any of the millions of men in the UK? This was worse than she thought.

'I think I need a glass of water.' Emily followed his instructions to the kitchen. Filling the glass from the tap, she bent over and drank greedily from it, only to refill it again. What had her mother been thinking? How could she have done this to a man she supposedly loved.

'Are you all right in there?'

Arnold's voice carried through into the kitchen.

'Yeah, I'm fine,' Emily called back.

Fine? But she was far from fine. On the edge more like.

She drank down the rest of the water and returned

to the living room determined to hear Arnold out with no interruptions.

'Sorry, Arnold, so as you were saying?'

'Clyde was convinced your mum had been having an affair. At first, he thought it was me,' Arnold gave a small laugh at the memory. 'Even tried to have a fight with me at one point.'

'So who was it then?' Emily asked, no longer able to contain herself.

'That's just it, Alice. There wasn't anyone else. Clyde is your dad. They must've given him the wrong test results. He refused to believe your mum, even after she offered to get a DNA test done, so she kicked him out, then made up all those lies about him and stopped him from seeing you. Regardless of all that, he still loved you both very much. It's just sad that he preferred to believe in his own paranoid thoughts right up until the very end.'

Emily didn't know what shocked her most, that her mum hadn't been unfaithful or that her dad had chosen to believe a misdiagnosis from his doctor.

'OK, if that's all true, why leave us penniless? If he loved us so much, how could he do that?'

Arnold frowned. 'What d'you mean? He always provided for you. Never missed a week of giving your mum money. He didn't shirk his responsibilities, whether your mum let him see you or not.'

Emily was speechless – which didn't happen often. All the poverty and misery they'd endured as children had just been a big game to their mother. Emily would keep this secret to herself. Their mother had done enough damage to Alice, she didn't want to hurt her anymore.

There was nothing Emily could do now, but at least she knew the truth. There had been no winners, and because of this mishap, they'd all had to suffer.

She looked at Arnold, coughing and spluttering into his handkerchief and knew it wouldn't be long before he'd be gone too. She'd be forever grateful that he'd been her dad's best friend and had remained loyal to him until the end.

Chapter Thirty-Six

Being a nurse, Kerry knew better than anyone not to jump to conclusions based on the expression on a doctor's face. Anything could have happened during the time the doctor had left her office to arrive at the ward. Her patient could have died, or she could have received bad news from home. At least Kerry hoped it was one of those things. Though she wasn't overly worried, she was nevertheless cautious. She knew bleeding happened to many women early in their pregnancy. If it was anything more serious, Kerry didn't think she'd be able to hold herself together.

Dr Cross looked down at her. 'The good news first, Congratulations on the baby, everything looks fine.'

Kerry released the breath she'd been holding for dear life. Almost instinctively, she placed her hand on her stomach and gave a silent prayer. She looked at Alice standing behind the doctor and saw she appeared as relieved as Kerry felt.

'What isn't so good is your blood pressure,' Dr Cross continued. 'It's unusually high. You need to take things easy, Kerry. Get your doctor to sign you off for a few weeks.'

'I will.' Kerry knew she couldn't risk disobeying the doctor's orders but if she didn't work, how was she going to earn a wage? If Kerry didn't sort something out quickly, she'd have to resort to selling her car and…

tears welled in her eyes, *Sarah's jewellery*.

Kerry barely noticed Dr Cross leave as she was too consumed in her thoughts for the future.

'You were right.'

Kerry eyed Alice.

'About being pregnant I mean. At least it's confirmed now. You've finally got what you want.'

Kerry fought back her tears. *Have I though?*

'You really shouldn't have come. I wouldn't have expected you to. Have you missed your flight?'

Alice nodded. Her expression was unreadable, making it hard for Kerry to sense how she felt. Pretty pissed off she imagined, especially seeing as it was a false alarm.

'Will you get a refund?'

'Probably not.'

Hearing this made Kerry feel even worse. It wasn't even as if she could pay some money towards a new ticket.

'I told Debbie not to call you.' Kerry paused. 'I feel terrible.'

Alice's features paled. 'Are you in pain? Do you want me to call the doctor back?'

'I'm fine, Alice,' Kerry said kindly, 'I was talking about you missing your flight.'

'Oh.' Alice's shoulders sagged slightly. 'Don't be. I'll sort something out.'

Kerry's heart sank to her stomach. So she was still intent on going. Why had Kerry assumed she wouldn't?

***

An hour later, Kerry was back home, Alice by her side.

'Let me get that,' Alice said, taking Kerry's keys to the front door.

Kerry laughed. 'I'm not an invalid. I can still use my hands.'

'The doctor said you need to rest.' Alice opened the door and gestured for Kerry to walk in first. 'Do you fancy a tea?'

'I'd love one, thank you.' Kerry lowered herself onto the sofa. All she wanted to do was curl up into a little ball and go to sleep. If Alice were to curl up behind her that would be a bonus, but she wouldn't press for her to stay. She'd done enough already by just being there.

'Here you go.' Alice walked back into the living room carrying a cup of tea. She placed it on the coffee table and to Kerry's relief, took her jacket off and sat down. She still felt a tad weak but she was grateful the dizziness she'd been experiencing had passed.

'Hey, I'm glad you're OK.'

'Me too.' Kerry reached over for her tea. It was warm and sickly sweet. Just what she needed.

'I think I'm going to have an early night,' Kerry said.

Though she didn't want Alice to go, Kerry also didn't want to get used to her presence. Better to end the suffering now than prolong the agony.

'Do you want me to stay over?'

Kerry shook her head. 'I'm sure you've got more interesting things to do than watch me sleep. Don't worry, I'll be fine. I am a nurse you know.'

'OK.'

As Alice stood, her phone rang and from the excited look on her face, she was happy to hear from the caller. Anxiety gnawed in Kerry's stomach not knowing who it was.

Alice was still talking on the phone as she slipped into her jacket. 'See you in twenty minutes, can't wait.'

Alice disconnected the call and faced Kerry. 'Are you sure you don't want me to stay?'

'Honestly, I'm fine.'

Alice bent over to kiss Kerry's cheek. 'Promise me you'll call me if there's an emergency.'

'I promise,' Kerry said, forcing a smile.

Kerry was disappointed that Alice hadn't made firm plans on whether or not they were going to see each other again. It was obvious her caller, whoever it was, was more important than Kerry.

The front door slammed, and Kerry lay down on the sofa, wrapping her arms around her stomach and speaking softly to the little one that was growing inside of her. 'It's just you and me now, and you're all I need.'

If that was true, why did Kerry feel like crying at the thought of having a future that didn't include Alice?

Chapter Thirty-Seven

Alice got to the bar earlier than Stella, so ordered a much-needed beer to steady her nerves. If her mind had been in turmoil before, she didn't know where it was at now. Standing in that hospital room waiting to hear the results of the baby's condition had been one of the scariest moments of her life. The relief she'd felt upon hearing the baby was OK was akin to winning the lottery.

Her feelings had come as a shock to her when she realised how much she cared about Kerry.

Care? Who am I kidding? I love her. Really love her in a way that makes me so scared I don't even want to admit it to myself, let alone Kerry.

As Alice battled her thoughts, she caught sight of Stella walking in. She looked around until she saw Alice's hand waving half-heartedly in the air.

Alice was taken aback by how different Stella looked as she neared. She was positively radiant. The lights from above glinted off her dark hair as she strode towards Alice in a confident manner. The vibrant energy she emitted was contagious.

Alice was on her feet in seconds, embracing her in a tight hug.

'I've missed you soooo much!'

'You too,' Stella said returning her hug with the same intensity.

They slowly drew apart and remained staring at one another as they sat down at the table.

'So how was it? Ten days of not talking. How did you manage it?'

'Quite easily. It was a relief actually. The worst part was the end when all the talking started up again. It made me realise how much unnecessary noise we have in our lives for no apparent reason other than to fill the silence.'

'Glass of wine?' Alice said, unable to take her eyes off her.

Stella shook her head. 'No thanks, I shan't be poisoning myself with alcohol anymore. I've seen the evil of my ways.'

There goes my drinking partner. 'Water?'

Stella suddenly burst out laughing. 'D'you think after living like a hermit for ten days on nothing but water and vegan food, I'd sit here and drink water. Fuck a glass, get a bottle of wine in.'

Alice laughed. It was great to have her friend back. Being with her now, it felt like a lifetime since she'd last seen her.

Once Alice returned from the bar and Stella had downed her first glass of wine in record speed, she looked at Alice in earnest.

'You seem stressed. You still worried about your mum?'

'No, so much has happened since you've been gone, I don't know where to start.'

'How about you pour me another glass and start at

the beginning.'

By the time Alice had finished telling Stella everything, Stella looked at her open-mouthed. 'Jesus Christ. So let me get this straight. You were meant to be on a plane flying to God knows where right this minute.'

Alice nodded.

'And you slept with your mum's nurse who is carrying her dead lover's baby?'

Alice nodded again.

'And your dad's best friend might be your dad?'

'Yep.'

'And your mum and Izzy.' Stella took a mouthful of wine. 'This is too much for my poor brain to take in.'

'Imagine how I feel. I'm the one that's got to live with myself.'

'So what do you want to do?'

'About what?'

'About the only thing you've got control over. You're relationship with Kerry.'

'What can I do?'

'Do you love her?'

Alice didn't have to think twice. She had already admitted it to herself. 'Yes, I do.'

'Then follow your heart, Alice. If these last ten days have taught me anything, it's that we need to allow happiness into our lives whenever it comes knocking, and if it leaves, allow it to go with the same grace we let it in with.'

'But the baby?'

'The baby is just another part of Kerry and you'll

love it in the same way. Don't throw it all away on an illusion. You think by travelling you're leaving your problems behind? Well, you're not. They'll be with you day and night until the end. Find yourself wherever you are. Whether that be with Kerry or on your own.'

'Does that mean you've made up your mind about your marriage to Fred?'

Stella smiled. 'Yes, I have and I'm staying for now. I have to find my own happiness in myself, not in anyone else. Not Fred, nor my child, not even you. My new journey's just beginning and I'm no longer wanting to know where it's going to end. I'm focusing on the path that I'm taking moment by moment.'

After fighting her feelings for such a long time, in the space of a few seconds, the decision that she was unable to make peace with finally made sense.

Alice left Stella soon after her epiphany as she could barely wait to speak to Kerry.

When her front door finally opened, Alice forgot what she was going to say at the sight of Kerry's puffy eyes.

She took a step towards her and gently stroked her cheek.

'What's the matter? Have you been bleeding again?'

Kerry shook her head, her eyes welling with tears as she backed away down the hallway. Alice followed her, shutting the door behind her.

'Why the tears?' Alice asked once they were sitting down in the living room.

'I just don't know how I'm going to do this on my

own.' Kerry let out a sob before burying her face in her hands. When she spoke, her words were barely audible. 'I thought we'd manage, just the two of us.'

Alice knelt beside her and gently prised Kerry's hands away from her face. 'The three of us you mean. And we will.'

Chapter Thirty-Eight

Eighteen months later

In the near distance, the golden reflection from the sun's rays danced idly on the white capped waves as they lapped towards the shore.

'One tequila sunrise for you and one for me,' Emily said, placing the bright orange drink on the table next to Alice.

Alice pushed herself into a sitting position on the sunbed and removed her sunglasses.

Letting out a satisfied breath, she turned to Emily as she made herself comfortable on the sunbed next to her. 'This is the life, isn't it?'

'It sure is,' Emily said, raising her glass. 'Cheers.'

'Here's to your future as a New York Times bestselling author. May your success continue.'

Emily grinned. 'I'll most definitely drink to that.'

Before Alice could take a sip, a hand came from behind her and expertly removed her drink. Alice glanced backwards and pouted when she came face to face with Kerry.

'I think it's your turn to change her nappy.'

'But you do it so well,' Alice said, pinching her nostrils with the tips of her fingers.

Kerry laughed at Alice's expression. 'Only because I change her most of the time.'

Wee, sick and snot Alice could handle but pooing was a no-no, despite how much space her love for Sarah took up in her heart.

Alice rose to her feet and followed Kerry into the apartment they had been renting in Mexico for the past six months. In the open plan living room, there were enough baby's toys to fill a small shop.

Baby Sarah lay on her back in a pen. Seeing Alice peek over the edge at her, she let out a loud squeal and gave Alice one of her gummy smiles. A smile that melted her heart every time she saw it.

Placing her finger into Sarah's tiny palm, the baby squeezed it with all her might. *Such innocence. Such perfection.* It was the adults that polluted their pure minds. Turned them into distrusting people with low self-esteem and a lack of self-worth.

Alice looked at the picture hanging on the wall and was struck by how much the baby looked like Sarah. She already had her red fiery hair and cute dimples.

Kerry playfully dangled a clean nappy in front of Alice's face and Alice laughed, batting it away.

'OK, I'll let you get away with it just this once.'

Alice encircled Kerry's waist with her arms. 'Have I told you how much I love you?'

'Yes, daily,' Kerry said, planting a kiss on Alice's lips before turning to tend to baby Sarah.

Alice looked on in awe at the way Kerry expertly removed the soiled nappy and cleaned Sarah with a baby wipe, all the while the pure love she felt for her emitting from her eyes. In return, Sarah giggled and gurgled as she stared up at the most amazing woman on the planet as far as Alice was concerned.

'You have got to stop being so prudish.' Emily came up behind Kerry, took the soiled nappy and placed it in a disposable bag.

'I will… one day.'

'Yeah, when's that? When Sarah's old enough to do it herself?' Emily said, joining in with the laughter resounding throughout the room.

What a difference eighteen months makes. The three women had bonded even more as a tight knit group in the months leading up to Sarah's birth.

When Alice had decided to stay and make her relationship work with Kerry, she had done so wholeheartedly. Following Stella's advice, Alice went to therapy and prepared herself for the birth of their beautiful baby, in the hope that she could provide her with a strong, loving, emotional connection she never received from her own mother.

It had been an interesting process. She had learnt much about Carol's behaviour and why she was the way she was. It wasn't easy for her to hear, but it gave her a better understanding of where things had gone wrong, which meant she could try and avoid those pitfalls. She still had contact with Carol, as did Emily. Since she'd moved to France to live with her sister, Carol hadn't been so demanding. They'd made a promise of building some sort of relationship via phone calls every few months as long as Carol didn't overstep the boundaries they'd put in place. Up until now, Carol had respected them.

All Alice knew was that in order for their relationship to survive, she would only be able to love her mother from afar. True love didn't involve co-dependency or attachment.

Alice picked Sarah up and held her close, gently kissing her cheek.

This was a new start for Alice. A new life. One where she would teach Sarah that true love doesn't have a happy ending.

True love has no ending.

The End

Printed in Great Britain
by Amazon

55449770R00168